"Hey, you!"
Capri snapped imperiously

She looked down at the man sprawled across the bed. "Does your boss pay you to sleep all afternoon? I don't have any water in my cabin."

The man might as well have been deaf; he didn't move a muscle.

Capri exhaled an angry breath. "And are we going to lie in bed all day?"

She heard a deep amused chuckle. "Honey, whatever you want. I'd intended to get up soon, but if you'd prefer..."

She jerked her gaze away and with a sweep of her arm that she hoped would convey the contempt that she felt for him, said, "If you're not over to my cabin in five minutes, I'll see that you're fired. And, I promise you, you'll never get a job as a caretaker anywhere in North America again!"

GRACE GREEN, born on a farm and brought up in the Scottish Highlands, says at heart, she's still a country girl. She was a teacher when she married her engineer husband, and after their third daughter arrived, they emigrated to Canada where their son, Gordon, was born. Her husband's work has taken them to many different places, from the Maritimes to the Queen Charlotte Islands and the Yukon. They are now happily settled in North Vancouver. Not until she read an article on romance writing several years ago did she realize this was what she wanted to do. Now she combines her favorite hobbies—reading, people-watching and scribbling—and her love of nature into doing what she loves best—writing and spinning dreams.

Books by Grace Green

GRACE GREEN

risk of the heart

Harlequin Books

TORONTO • NEW YORK • LONDON
AMSTERDAM • PARIS • SYDNEY • HAMBURG
STOCKHOLM • ATHENS • TOKYO • MILAN
MADRID • WARSAW • BUDAPEST • AUCKLAND

For Jilly

Harlequin Presents first edition July 1992
ISBN 0-373-11475-3

Original hardcover edition published in 1991
by Mills & Boon Limited

RISK OF THE HEART

CHAPTER ONE

WAS her father *never* going to give up?

Capri Jones slumped back in her swivel chair, her gray-green eyes sparking with frustration as she glared at the three brochures on her desk—brochures which had just been delivered to her penthouse office at Jones Oil.

She wove her fingers restlessly through the chocolate-brown hair that hung like a skein of silk to her shoulders... and for once the hint of Must de Cartier pulsing from the delicate skin at her inner wrist didn't give her any pleasure.

The time had come, she decided with a compressing of her lips, to put a stop to it! Her patience had——

The buzz of the intercom shattered her thoughts, and with a terse exclamation she depressed the flashing plastic button. "Yes, Gabby?"

"Overseas call, Ms. Jones. Your dad. Line one."

"Thanks." Inhaling a deep, calming breath, Capri kicked off her Bruno Magli pumps, and, tucking her feet under the chair, lifted the phone.

"Hi, Jake." Her tone was casual, but the fingertips of her left hand tapped out a soft, deliberate tattoo on the surface of her desk. "How's the situation in Venezuela?"

"Everything's under control, thank heavens. Three of the producing wells were on fire, but Garson was magnificent. He managed to close the bottom master valves on all eight producing wells—had to crawl into the fire to do it, under a water shield——"

"Wonderful." Quickly Capri moved to cut him off. She had worked at Jones Oil, her father's Houston-based company, since she had graduated from university at twenty-one, and the only facet of the industry she disliked hearing about was oil well fires. She shuddered. She disliked hearing about *fires*, period... Her heart clenched as her mind suddenly became a collage of vivid and painful images, and, with a skill born of long and anguished practice, she demolished them and redirected her thoughts. "Are you going on to Australia now?"

"Leaving tomorrow." Despite the static on the overseas line, her father's voice came through brusque and clear. "Tell me, did Peerless Vacations send you the brochures?"

Capri's toes curled like pincers into the plush cream carpet. Easy now, she warned herself... "They did." Her gaze skated icily over the vividly colored brochures: the cover of the first depicted a rugged Scottish castle, the second a luxurious Spanish hacienda, and the third a sprawling Californian ranch. "I have them right here in front of me."

"Good. Now all you have to do is study the pictures, pick the one that appeals to you most, book in for a couple of weeks and enjoy your holiday."

"Jake, thanks, but——"

"No need to thank me..." There was a rustle at the other end of the line, and Capri felt her blood-pressure rise a couple of notches as she pictured her father flourishing his cigar dismissively—a characteristic gesture, and one which, she'd learned years ago, meant he was putting an end to whatever matter had been under discussion. "Now, Cappy, I'm going to be incommunicado till the end of the month while I'm trekking around in the outback. I'll see you when I get home— I'll be back in Houston before the board meeting on September third——"

Capri lurched to her feet. "Jake, *listen to me.*" Standing ramrod straight, she squared her shoulders under the authoritative pads of her green linen jacket and went on adamantly, "You can forget about the brochures. Up till now, I've always spent my summer vacation at one of the places you've picked out for me. *I don't want to do that any more.* This year, I want to choose my own spot." She tilted her chin stubbornly. "It may come as a surprise to you, but I guessed a long time ago what you were trying to do, and I just won't——"

There was a click and the line went dead.

For a second, Capri froze, unable to believe what had happened. Then, spitting out a venomous, "Damn!" she crashed the receiver back into its cradle. Scooping up the three brochures, she whirled them wildly into the air, and in her stockinged feet began pacing back and forth across the room.

She was twenty-five and her father was *still* pulling the strings as he had since she was a toddler! He was taking advantage of the fact that she would do anything to please him—or almost anything, she amended with a bitter twist of her lips. Why did he *persist* in sending her each summer to vacation spots where he knew there would be wealthy, eligible men—wealthy, eligible men she would spend her whole holiday trying to avoid?

Why couldn't he understand that she didn't want to get married?

It was one of the few things they ever argued about. Jake desperately wanted his daughter to marry and provide him with a grandchild...and Capri refused to cooperate. She had never been able to bring herself to explain her reasons. How could she, without talking about her mother and Jamie? And she never, ever talked about her mother or her twin brother. Not with anyone. Not even with Jake. It hurt too much——

Capri came to a halt suddenly, a frown tugging her brow. When she'd flung the brochures into the air, one had landed wrong side up on the carpet...and a small photo was tucked against the back of it with a paper clip... It must have caught there accidentally, she mused. She bent down to retrieve it.

It was a black and white snap of a modest log cabin. Curiously, she turned it over, to find that someone had scribbled on the back in pencil.

Doubt if any of our clients would be interested in renting this godforsaken little place, one of several on a small island off the coast of British Columbia, Canada. Please phone Bill at Spartan's Lo-Cost Holidays and tell him thanks but no, thanks...

There followed a phone number, and the message was signed "Anton."

Capri smiled wryly as she sat down again and tossed the picture on her desk. Whoever "Anton" was, he was right...none of the people who hired Peerless Vacations to arrange the ultimate holiday for them would be interested in this little cabin. Like oil tycoon Jake Jones, Peerless Vacations clients were all multimillionaires who expected to be pampered and entertained while on vacation.

There would be no theaters on this island, no gambling casinos, no exclusive stores. No high-class restaurants where handsome men in impeccable dinner jackets could dazzle the sophisticated women of their choice with gourmet food, champagne, and a wonderful band playing romantic music in the background while——

Capri's breath hissed in sharply as she backed her thoughts up. On this little island, there would be no handsome men in impeccable dinner-jackets!

An idea began to sprout in her brain—an idea which was so ridiculous that she gave her head an abrupt shake in an attempt to clear it. Yet a moment later she found herself bending forward, her elbows on the desk, as she looked at the black and white photo again. More closely this time. And, very cautiously, she let the idea begin to sprout once more.

When it was in full bloom, she leaned back in her chair and, toying with her chunky gold earrings, stared unseeingly through the slats of the venetian blinds at the hazy Houston skyline. Jake's voice echoed in her head, "...Study the pictures...pick the one that appeals most..."

She could feel a chuckle rising from way down inside her chest.

Eyes alight with laughter, she reached for the phone and dialed the number scrawled on the back of the photo.

When a woman answered with a businesslike, "Spartan's Lo-Cost Holidays, Lynette speaking," she responded in a voice that was rich with amusement,

"Hi, Lynette. My name is Capri Jones. I'd like to talk with Bill..."

"There's your island, lady...and this is Blueberry Cove."

Capri nodded vaguely, barely hearing the soft voice of the Native American youth as he cut the engine of the boat and allowed it to drift toward the jetty, where several other small craft bobbed with the waves and pulled against their moorings. She was too busy with her own thoughts...

She had finally outfoxed her father!

There would be no dinner-jacketed high-rollers lurking on this small, remote island, no eligible bachelors intent on luring her into marriage. For two whole weeks, she'd be able to do her own thing without interruption—and yet she'd followed Jake's instructions to the letter!

She looked lovingly at the laptop computer tucked on the seat beside her, next to her case, and gave it a little pat. If she did her homework, she would give Jake a big surprise at the September board meeting. He had been concerned about the high degree of absenteeism at the Houston office during the past year; unknown to him, she'd had the personnel department do extensive research into the problem. She had brought the files with her, and hoped that during the next two weeks she could study the statistics, and come up with some valuable suggestions as to how the situation could be remedied.

"...caretaker's cabin. And you're in number one, up there above the beach."

Capri started. "Sorry, I was dreaming. Oh, yes, I see my cabin... And the caretaker's...where...?"

"Behind those trees." The boy gestured toward a curved line of evergreens a stone's throw from the beach. "If no one's around, help yourself to anything you need."

"Oh." Capri smiled, and, unfastening her orange life jacket, shrugged it off. "I will."

A few moments later, she was standing on the wooden structure, computer slung over her shoulder, case by her side.

"Thanks," she called. The youth raised his hand fleetingly, then, aiming his attention toward the other side of the inlet, started up his motor; soon the sound was receding in the distance.

Capri picked up her case and walked slowly along the jetty, looking around her as she went. The island, which was about a mile in length, rose out of the ocean with the shape of a gigantic egg. Though the northern portion was heavily forested, the rest must have been cleared at some time, for it was covered by stumps and scrub and long grass. A sandy white beach ribboned this eastern shore, and on its fringe, just twenty yards from the jetty, was the small log building which was to be her home for the next two weeks. It stood alone. The caretaker's cabin wasn't visible from here...and Capri guessed her own cabin would be shielded from it by the branches of the trees. Good, she thought...

A blue jay flew chattering over her head as she climbed up the three steps carved into the rock at her front door, and she felt an unfamiliar lightness of her heart as she turned the key that was in the lock, and stepped inside.

She found herself in a tiny, bright kitchen, with a wooden table against one wall, and two bentwood chairs. Through an arch to the left, she could see a small living room furnished colonial-style, its window looking out over the ocean. She placed her computer on the kitchen table, and moved across to explore the bedroom, which also opened off the kitchen. It smelled dry and dusty, and contained a single bed, a pine dresser with a woven green mat, and a pine bedside table with tobacco burns along its edge.

It wasn't what she was used to, but—Capri shrugged her shoulders—who cared? Roughing it might be fun. And she couldn't have wished for a more peaceful place. It was so quiet that through the open window she could hear the soft slip-slap as the wavelets licked the wooden jetty.

Two whole weeks, a perfect setting in which to do her work, and nothing—and nobody—to distract her.

Throwing her case on the green and tangerine check bedspread, she tugged the zipper open ... and felt her carefree mood dissipate abruptly as she reached for the silver-framed photo lying on top of her silk nightshirt. A photo of Jamie—his blond hair disheveled, his mouth crooked in a heart-tugging smile, his chin set at a determined angle...his laughing blue eyes mirroring that same determination. Capri gripped the portrait of her twin brother tightly, feeling her heart ache.

Eyes blurred, she traced the tip of one finger over the inscription: "To my other half." She remembered the day he'd scribbled the words. Remembered it only too well. He'd left that afternoon for Europe, to compete in the car race which had claimed his life.

Sometimes she thought she must be crazy, to keep the picture always by her bedside, taking it with her when she traveled, for each time she looked at it she felt as if a giant fist was pummeling her heart.

But the portrait served its purpose: it kept fresh in her mind the agony she had felt when she had watched her brother die—die so horribly. And it kept just as fresh her vow never to let herself fall in love, and let herself become vulnerable to that kind of anguish again.

Biting her lower lip to stop its trembling, she set the photo carefully on her bedside table, and resolutely began to unpack.

"Damn!" Capri glowered frustratedly at the kitchen tap. "When you're turned on, water's supposed to come out!"

She looked at her watch. She'd already wasted far too much time with the darned thing—let the caretaker deal with it. He might at least have seen to it that she had a water supply. Irritably, she replaced the lid on the jar of Maxwell House coffee, and stalked to the door.

The hot sun burned on her bare shoulders and the knee-high grass tickled her bare legs as she marched toward the caretaker's cabin. As she reached the trees, and passed between two large pines, she saw the small log building just ahead, at the end of a narrow sun-baked path.

The door was ajar, and after knocking lightly she stood for a moment, listening to the answering silence with her head cocked to one side. No, it wasn't complete silence... there *was* a sound from inside—but it was one she couldn't identify... a regular, droning noise.

She rapped on the door again, this time with more force, and when there was still no response she called out briskly, "Is anyone home?"

The droning continued uninterrupted, and, frowning, Capri pushed the door open with her fingertips.

The kitchen was empty. As was the living room. With her nerves twitching, Capri tiptoed toward the open bedroom door and looked in.

Oh, dear Lord...

Leaning one hand against the doorframe for support, she found herself almost overcome by a devastating sense of *déjà vu*. On the double bed lay a man, sprawled face down—a man who looked so like Jamie that she thought for a moment that she must be dreaming.

How many times had she looked in on a similar scene before...at a powerfully built, tautly muscled figure lying pole axed on top of the covers, head buried in the pillows? The sound she had heard was snoring; now that she was in the same room it sounded much louder, much more intense, as if it came from someone who intended never to wake up again.

Capri shuddered, and determinedly banished the eerie feeling that she was looking at her brother. Now that she'd had time to look properly, she could see that this man was a good four inches taller than Jamie had been, and even more powerfully built. And whereas her twin had been twenty-one when he had died this man appeared to be in his mid-thirties.

His hair was blond as a Californian surfer's, and it tousled untidily against his strong neck, contrasting sharply with the deep mahogany brown of his skin. He was wearing nothing but a pair of well-worn khaki shorts, and Capri felt her pulse quicken as her gaze lingered a moment longer than necessary on muscular legs that were generously covered with dark gold hair.

His right arm was flung out to one side, his left hung over the edge of the double bed, and Capri's upper lip curled with distaste as she saw that dangling precariously from the long, hard fingers was a beer can.

"Hey, you!" she snapped imperiously. "Does your boss pay you to sleep all afternoon? Would you mind getting up? I don't have any water!"

The man on the bed might just as well have been deaf; he didn't move a muscle.

Capri exhaled an angry breath, and placed her hands on her hips. "Look, if you don't get up right now, I'll...I'll..."

Just what *could* she do? With a darkly muttered exclamation, she looked around her for something to poke him with. There was nothing. Apart from a large pair of Reebok running shoes which had been flung down by the dresser along with a crumpled khaki cotton shirt, the room was bare. Frowning, she turned to stare at him again——

And found herself looking into one blue eye that was fixed on her with sleep-dazed wonder. Its owner still had his head buried in the pillow, with the other eye still hidden, but he'd twisted his face around a couple of inches so that he could see her. He took his sweet time in running his gaze over her. Over her glossy brown hair, her flushed cheeks, and her pursed, cherry-painted lips, before moving more slowly over the blue jersey tube top which barely contained her full, high breasts, and the perky white shorts that revealed her trim waist and the feminine curve of her hips...

She heard him sigh. And the ecstatic sound was immediately followed by an equally ecstatically murmured, "Lord be praised. I've died and gone to heaven..."

His words were muffled into the pillow, but Capri had no problem making them out. She had also no problem interpreting the blatantly suggestive tone in which they were couched.

What she did have a problem doing was concentrating. She could now see enough of his face—despite the several days' growth of tough blond beard—to realize that the caretaker of the Blueberry Cove Cabins was an absolute hunk. His brow was intelligent and strong, his nose perfectly chiseled...and as he twisted around another inch she admitted sourly that his mouth was the kind just made for whispering sweet nothings into a woman's ear. It was wide, sensual, and at the moment crinkled in the laziest, cockiest smile she'd ever seen in her life.

She cleared her throat, wriggling uncomfortably in a vain effort to rid herself of the prickly sensations that had started dancing across her skin. "And are we going to lie in bed all day?" she asked, injecting into her voice all the sarcasm she could dredge up.

She heard a deep, amused chuckle. "Honey, whatever you want. I'd intended getting up soon, but if you'd prefer..."

Drawing herself up to her full height of five feet five inches, Capri bestowed on him the kind of look she usually reserved for something left in the fridge long enough to grow fungus. "Would you please tell me," she pronounced each word slowly and with icy precision, "how a person can make a cup of coffee if that person doesn't have any water?"

The beer can clattered hollowly on the pine floor and there was a scratching sound as tanned fingers scraped against a bristled jaw. "Got me on that one, I'm afraid. Never was much good at Trivial Pursuit." He rolled lazily onto his back and the muscles of his arms rippled then bunched as he rearranged the pillow under his head. The one perfect blue eye, thickly fringed with surprisingly dark lashes, was now joined by its equally perfect, equally amused mate.

"I have no water in my cabin."

Capri had thought him magnificently built when all she could see was his back view; now she found herself licking suddenly parched lips as she was treated to the sight of a wide chest with crisp golden curls, a tautly muscled stomach with darker blond hair V-ing down into the waistband of the khaki shorts...

She jerked her gaze away, and, with a sweep of her arm that she hoped would convey all the contempt she felt for him, said, "If you're not over at my cabin—that's cabin number one—in five minutes, I'll see that you're fired. And, I promise you, you'll never get a job as a caretaker anywhere in North America again!"

There, she thought triumphantly as she sailed from the room, that should show him. Lazy he might be, and irresponsible too, but he'd have to be stupid to risk losing this job—which appeared to be a very cushy one—and he didn't *look* stupid.

What he *did* look was irresistible, sexy, and devastatingly masculine, and beneath that sleepy exterior she had sensed a coiled-up challenge—a sexual challenge. His laid-back attitude hadn't fooled her for a minute. If she'd given him one whit of encouragement, he'd have whisked her right into that bed with him. And right now she would be lying there, with her slender frame pulled up tightly against that glorious and lithe-looking body——

Capri shivered, and came to a full stop. Glorious and lithe-looking body indeed! Good grief, what was she dreaming about? The man was a *caretaker*!

But not a very good one, she reminded herself as she grimly began walking again. And if he didn't turn up at her cabin before the deadline she'd given him he wouldn't be a caretaker for very much longer.

She looked at her watch and started counting.

He made it with four seconds to spare.

Capri peeked from behind the befrilled and flower-sprigged plastic curtains at her kitchen window as he walked up the path to her door...

No, not walked. Swaggered. As if he owned the very ground over which he strode. He was far too self-confident, she decided with a thin compressing of her lips, for his own good. Well, she hadn't risen to her senior administrative post at Jones Oil by letting people intimidate her. She'd better show this caretaker right away just what his place was in the scheme of things!

When she looked around he was standing in the doorway, blocking out the light. He was, she realized with dismay, even taller and leaner than she'd judged him to be. And harder... And sexier-looking than any man had a right to be!

Thumbs tucked inside the waistband of his jeans, he slanted his lips in a disarming smile and drawled, "Here I am, ma'am, at your service."

"What's your name?" Her voice—considering the dismay still coursing through her!—was gratifyingly curt.

He leaned lazily against the door jamb before answering. "Smith. Taggart Smith." His gaze dropped to her long legs, and she saw one corner of his mouth twitch in an appreciative smile. When he looked up again, his eyes were bluer than any she'd ever seen before. "And yours?"

Irritation surged through Capri as she felt electrical tinglings jump across her nerve-endings. "Jones," she snapped.

"Jones." He pushed himself from the wooden frame. "That's it?"

"That's it," she retorted. "Just Jones!"

"Short for something? Justine?"

Who'd have guessed she was going to be stuck with a smart aleck for a caretaker? "I meant," she said in acid tones, "you can call me Ms. Jones."

"*Ms.* Jones." He half closed his eyes, as if he were considering it. Then, after a moment or two, he shook his head. "Doesn't sound right. Too formal for island living. Maybe I'll cut out the Ms. and stick with Jones. It has a certain ring to it."

He came toward her—towering over her—and he smelled of the ocean, and the earth, and a male, musky scent that was so intense, so intoxicating that it seemed to drug her senses. Then he moved lazily past, and her breath caught in her throat as his forearm skimmed past her hip.

It was like being singed by a white-hot coal, she thought as she stumbled back. He appeared not to have noticed her reaction, and was fiddling with a contraption under the window, pumping it up and down. As she watched, she saw water dribbling from the tap. And a moment later it came out in a steady gush.

A blush started at her neck and worked its way swiftly up over her cheeks. So the water had to be pumped first... Why hadn't she explored a little, before rushing off for help? Next time, she'd know better, she decided.

When he finally cut the water off and turned around to face her, she expected a smug, "What was the problem?" Instead, he said in a matter-of-fact tone, "Sorry about that. Used to be instructions posted here above the sink. Wonder what happened to them? I'll have to see the..." He cleared his throat, and began again, "I'll have to see to it."

"Thanks." The word came out clearly, but with a grudging edge to it. Why didn't he leave? she wondered impatiently, as he began wandering around the kitchen, knocking on walls, opening cupboard doors. It was on the tip of her tongue to tell him to get out, but he *had* been tactful——

"Some work to be done here, I'm afraid." He banged his fist on the wall close by the door. "Termites. Pacific damp wood termites. There was a planter outside, right against this wall, and there wasn't proper drainage... This cabin was supposed to be fixed up before it was let again. Must have been a slip-up in communications with Spartan's Lo-Cost. I'll try not to get in your way, Jones, but I'm afraid I'm going to be underfoot quite a bit."

"But——"

"Yes?" He raised his blond eyebrows, and fixed her with an innocent gaze.

"It's just that..." Capri stopped. Why had she let herself become so defensive? "I have work to do," she said coldly. "I was banking on being left alone. That's why I came here."

"Ah. For peace and quiet. What's your line of work?"

"I'm..." The automatic words died in her throat. She didn't want this man, or any of the other people on the island, to know who she was. It had always embarrassed her that she had so much, though she had worked long and hard to achieve her position at Jones Oil. After all, she'd had the advantage of being born with a silver spoon stuck firmly in her mouth, an advantage that someone like Taggart Smith would probably resent. Nothing about her gave away her financial situation—the clothes she'd brought with her were mainly casual cotton things, and she'd left her good jewelery at home. The only item of value in her possession was her computer. It was still on the kitchen table, and now she found herself looking at it helplessly...and praying for inspiration.

His gaze followed hers, and he nodded. "You're a writer?"

"Yes," she said quickly. "That's it. A writer."

He walked to the door, turning on the step. "What do you write?"

Say something, she told herself, anything, just get him out of here! He really was having a very odd effect on her. There was something about the way he moved, something about that cocky twist of his lean hips, the arrogance of his stride, that stirred an unfamiliar and disturbing excitement in her blood. It was absolutely ridiculous! It couldn't be happening, this involuntary chemical reaction. Certainly he was a gorgeous-looking specimen, but she was an heiress to millions, while he was only a caretaker...

The situation, she realized wryly, was similar to those found in a true confession magazine. Or between the pages of a romantic novel. The blurb almost wrote itself.

"She was a Texan heiress, but the man whose body sent shivers down her spine was only a ne'er-do-well caretaker."

And at that very moment Capri felt a surge of the inspiration for which she'd been praying just moments before.

She took in a deep breath and crossed her fingers behind her back before uttering one of the few lies she had ever told in her life. "I write romances."

Taggart Smith did a double-take, his blue eyes so astonished that Capri almost laughed aloud. She managed to control the urge, and, without giving him time to reply, crossed to the door and slammed it shut in his face.

CHAPTER TWO

CAPRI watched from behind the plastic curtains till the tall, infuriatingly self-assured figure disappeared beyond the line of trees that sheltered his cabin. With a bit of luck, she thought, as she pumped water into the kettle, she wouldn't see him again today; it was rather late in the afternoon for someone to start tearing apart walls—even termite-infested walls. And especially when that someone was as lazy as Taggart Smith appeared to be.

He had probably gone straight back to bed!

Dismissing him abruptly from her mind, she rummaged in the drawer by the sink for matches, and, lighting one of the rings on the gas stove, put the kettle on. Then, with her bottom perched on the edge of the sturdy wooden table, she looked around the kitchen as she waited for the water to boil.

What would Jake think if he could see her now? she wondered mischievously. Her gaze flickered over the heavy-duty linoleum with its faded pink and blue mosaic pattern, over the rough-hewn pine cupboards, over the propane gas stove and the ancient fridge with its slightly rusty handle. She frowned as her glance settled on a small Franklin wood stove that stood in the corner adjacent to the bedroom door. For heating the cabin at night? Did it get that cold here after the sun went down? No need to worry, though...beside it, she noticed, there was a reassuring pile of logs. Enough to last her——

She stiffened as she heard a soft scrabbling sound at the door, then, as she heard it again, her pulse quickened. Surely that darned caretaker hadn't come back? Well, she decided firmly as she slid her bottom from the edge

of the table, if he had, she would tell him his Pacific
damp wood termites would just have to wait!

Her sandals flip-flopped over the lino as she strode to
the door. Pausing for a moment, she schooled her features into disapproving lines, and then, snatching the
handle abruptly, swung open the door.

For a fraction of a second, she thought she must have
been mistaken; there was nobody there. Then a flash of
blue at her feet drew her gaze down, and she saw a dainty
toddler in an azure one-piece swimsuit scrambling up
her steps—a little girl with a mass of carroty curls and
a freckled elfin face.

Capri breathed a sigh of relief, and relaxed. This kind
of visitor she could enjoy!

She realized she was being warily examined by a pair
of inquisitive green eyes, and she crouched down in the
doorway. "Hi," she said softly. "What's your name?"

"Name."

With a chuckle, Capri touched one of the child's
copper-bright curls. "Where's your Mom? Are
you——?"

"Miranda, honey! I've told you before, that's not our
cabin! Let's—oh!" The cheerful, exasperated voice broke
off as its owner realized Miranda wasn't alone. Capri
straightened. A young woman was coming around the
corner, a woman so like the little girl that she had to be
her mother—and her bulky shape left Capri in no doubt
that Miranda was due to have a baby brother or sister
in the not too far distant future.

"I'm sorry if Miranda disturbed you—all the cabins
on the island look the same and she thinks each one is
home! We're on our way to the beach." The young
woman gestured with the huge straw bag she carried; it
was brimming with spade, pail, beach ball and towels.
Her delicate features crinkled in a smile as she went on,
"I'm Ellen Walters. My husband Sam and I—and
Miranda—are in cabin three, just over the hilltop."

"Hi." Capri found herself warming to the other woman's open friendliness. "I'm Capri Jones." She shaded her eyes from the late afternoon sun as she glanced down toward the beach. "It's a gorgeous day, isn't it?"

"Heavenly." The other woman hesitated. "You're not alone, are you?"

"As a matter of fact, I am."

"Would you like to join us?" the other woman asked eagerly. "Sam's having a nap, and I'd love some company. We've been here for a week and I'm dying to talk with another female—Miranda's one-word sentences aren't exactly conducive to satisfactory conversations! We could all have a swim first, if you like."

Capri looked at the sparkling waves. She could feel her tube top sticking clammily to her back, feel sweat pooling between her breasts—it would be refreshing to cool off in the ocean before she started working on her report. "I——"

"Tiger!" Miranda's delighted shout interrupted Capri just as she was about to accept Ellen's invitation. The little girl clambered down the steps and began toddling away along the path, and as Capri looked to see where she was going she saw Taggart Smith's already familiar figure walking toward the beach, his body looking more tanned than ever in contrast with the dazzling white trunks he was wearing—brief, low-slung trunks that even at a distance of over twenty yards left little to the imagination.

Hurriedly averting her gaze, Capri drew back inside. "Thanks, Ellen. I really haven't time——"

Just before she closed the door, she saw a flicker of hurt in Ellen's green eyes, and she clicked her tongue with vexation. She hadn't intended to offend the other woman, yet she obviously had. But what had been the alternative? she wondered helplessly as she leaned back against the door. To walk down to the beach in one of her bikinis, with Taggart Smith's suggestive blue gaze mocking her? The very thought made her shiver.

What was it about the man that he had managed to get under her skin...and so swiftly? She had always been very comfortable around the opposite sex—had had to be, in the business she was in! But Taggart Smith was different from her colleagues at Jones Oil. Those ambitious young men were impeccably groomed, and smelled as if they'd just been sampling colognes at some exclusive boutique...whereas the caretaker of Blueberry Island Cabins looked like a beachcomber and smelled of the earth and the ocean—and if any company could bottle his tantalizing musky male scent, Capri decided with a self-derisive twist of her lips, it would triple its cologne sales overnight.

Without her conscious consent, her feet carried her to the window. Her fingers parted the plastic curtains, and her eyes scanned the beach to see where the caretaker had gone. Not very far, she realized with an unprecedented lurch of her heart—he had joined up with Ellen and Miranda. Ellen had spread out two huge beach towels on the sand, and she and Taggart were strolling toward the water, swinging Miranda between them. Capri heard the child's little squeals of delight as her feet splashed into the water.

Despite the bright sunshine, Capri felt the day had suddenly become darker. As she tugged the plastic curtains sharply together again, shutting out the happy scene on the beach, she was overcome by a feeling of loneliness.

Restlessly, she paced the small kitchen, her thoughts all of a jumble.

She had never met a man who disturbed her peace of mind the way Taggart Smith did. But then she had never met a man who could set her heart pounding, her pulses racing, from a distance of more than twenty yards...

Had she made a terrible mistake, she asked herself distractedly, in coming to this beautiful and remote island?

The only reply to her question was the urgent shrill of the whistling kettle as the water came to the boil, and, with a weary sigh, she hurried to lift it from the stove.

The sun went down around nine o'clock. Within minutes, it seemed, the cabin became cold and gloomy, and as Capri raised her eyes from her computer screen and looked toward the window she was surprised to see that the sky—which had been gloriously pink and silver the last time she'd glanced out—was now a dusky navy color.

With an anxious exclamation, she saved the work she'd just entered, and switched off the computer. To her relief she found that the Franklin stove was already set with kindlers and crisp newspapers; within moments of her touching a match to the paper the fire was sparking furiously and yellow flames were licking the dry logs and sending out welcome warmth.

Carefully shutting the little door, Capri prowled around the kitchen in the half light, opening cupboards, hoping to find a lamp. There had to be one, she told herself firmly. Her search, however, was fruitless. What was she going to——?

"Jones!" The loud voice, and a peremptory knock on the cabin door, broke into her distracted thoughts, making her jump. Before she could answer, she heard the rattle of the door handle—heard, again, a demanding "Jones!"

"Yes, Mr. Smith?" she snapped. "What do you want?"

"I noticed there was no light showing from your window and I thought maybe you hadn't found the lamp."

Capri put her hands on her hips. "I haven't."

"It should be on the floor—right behind the wood-pile."

Hurrying across the kitchen, Capri leaned over the pile of logs and in the purple shadows saw what she was looking for. She grabbed the lamp by the handle and, swinging it up, set it on the table. "Thanks," she called out coolly. "I've got it."

"Do you know how to light it?"

Capri hesitated, torn between a desire to be rid of him and the realization that if she didn't accept his help she'd have to sit in darkness till she went to bed. "No," she muttered grimly, "I don't."

"What did you say?" There was a mocking edge to his voice.

"No," she said loudly. "I don't know how to light the damned thing!" She stamped over to the door, and, unlocking it, stepped aside. "Come in," she invited dourly.

"Thank you, Jones."

Capri moved back as he brushed past her.

"I see you've got the stove going." His lazy glance sent shivers skating across her skin. "Stoke it up before you go to bed—it'll take the chill off the cabin in the morning. The air here can sometimes get pretty cold at night, this time of year."

She watched wordlessly as he worked to get the lamp going. But though she tried to focus her attention on his deft fingers she found herself mesmerized by the play of the flickering shadows on the bearded planes of his jaw, and by the rich gleam of gold in his thick, silky hair.

"There," he murmured at last, "that's it. And when it's time for bed . . ."

He looked around suddenly as he spoke, and he stopped short, as if taken aback that she was standing so close. She hadn't realized she'd moved nearer as she watched him, and she too was caught unawares. Their eyes met, and locked, and a shiver of electricity passed between them with such intensity that Capri felt as stunned as if he had hit her over the head with a sledgehammer.

"When it's time for bed——" he made the words sound like an invitation "—you can turn it off. This is the valve..."

Capri's long hair fell forward as she craned her head over to see what he was pointing at; fell forward perilously close to the lamp's lambent flame. But, in the fraction of a second before she could act, before she could flick it away, Taggart took charge.

"Careful!" His voice was no longer a drawl, but a sharp command, as his long capable fingers captured the silky strands in a swift blur of movement and brushed them away from danger.

Capri stepped back from him. "Thanks." Her voice had a distinct tremor. She was always so very wary around fire. What had this man done to her to make her so careless?

The cabin had seemed small earlier, now it seemed claustrophobic. And with the lamp bathing the room in gold, and the cozy glow and gentle crackle from the wood stove, an air of intimacy permeated the air, a closeness that seemed to draw the breath from Capri's lungs.

He was wearing a navy flannel shirt, and a pair of worn jeans. One of the buttons of his shirt was missing, she noted absently, and the front hung open almost to the waist. He had the kind of chest that any female would want to cuddle against—broad, muscled, and tanned——

"Meet with your approval?"

Capri cursed silently. Damn the man! She'd never met anyone so unnerving. But then she wasn't used to anyone quite so blunt. Or quite so sure of himself. His question had been amused, as if he already knew the answer...

"My approval?" She curled her lip haughtily. "Why should you care if your body meets with my approval?"

"Oh, I think you already know the answer to that." He chuckled.

"No," she retorted, "I certainly don't. Would you like to enlighten me?"

He cocked his head to one side, and curved his lips in a slow, sensual smile that did the strangest things to her heart. "Perhaps you really don't know. Perhaps you're not quite ready to know...not yet. But there's plenty of time. You're here for two weeks."

Capri felt as if her head was spinning. What on earth did he mean? Ready to know what? But before she could come up with an answer he spoke again.

"How's the story going?"

The sudden change of subject made Capri's head spin even faster. Story? What story?

And then, as she saw his glance flicker to her computer, she remembered the little white lie she'd told him the first time he'd come to the cabin—that she wrote romances! Since then she hadn't given it another thought.

"Oh..." She shrugged. "Oh, all right...I guess."

"What's the problem? Got writer's block?" He propped his hip on the edge of the table. "Want to discuss your plot? Sometimes that can help to get things straight in your mind—just talking about it."

Capri tried to direct the conversation off at a tangent. "You seem to know how to tackle the problem! Are you friendly with any writers?"

Now it was his turn to shrug. "Oh, I've met one or two in my day. Tell me, Jones..." his blue eyes were curious "...what's the storyline?"

So he wasn't to be easily diverted. In that case... "Oh, I'm not having any problem with the storyline." Capri's gaze met his steadily. "It's about a career woman who goes on holiday to a remote cabin where she hopes she will be left alone to get on with her work, only to find there's a fly in the ointment——''

"Aah," Taggart's response was a long-drawn-out drawl. "An interesting situation. This fly," she could tell he was trying hard not to laugh, "does he have a name?"

"Not yet." Capri waved an airy hand. "I'd thought of Mike, or Chris, or Andrew—but these names have such nice connotations, and there's nothing nice about this man. He's abrasive, aggressive, lazy, annoying, and cocky. He is, in essence, a pest. And I want a name that will convey this to the reader——''

"Feel free to use mine." The laughter he'd obviously been trying so hard to contain finally escaped to roll out infectiously. "He sounds like an absolute bastard, and Taggart will suit him perfectly."

Capri quirked one dark eyebrow in mock surprise. "Why, so it does." Her tone was dismissive. With a gesture in the direction of the door, she started to walk toward it.

He didn't budge. "Now," he mused, scratching one hand over his roughly stubbled jaw, "the career woman. She is, I take it, young—probably in her mid-twenties—and extremely attractive, with silky brown hair and intense gray-green eyes, and the kind of figure the designer of the first bikini must have had in mind. Not a Prudence; certainly not a Violet or a Chastity..." He snapped his fingers. "Eureka. She has got to be called——''

"Her name is Capri." Turning the door handle, Capri flung the door open and swiveled around to face him. "And what she looks like in a bikini is none of your damned business——''

"Now that you have the names sorted out in your mind," he said smoothly as he slid his hip from the table, "you'll probably be able to get a better handle on the characters. These two seem like very strong people who both know exactly what they want. Sparks are going to fly! I think you're trying too hard. If you just sit back and let things happen between them, you'll be surprised at the result.''

Capri gripped the edge of the door tightly as he walked toward her. Blue velvet. His eyes looked like blue velvet. Deep and rich and seductive. She'd never before met a man who could invite her to make love without even saying one word... "Good night, Mr. Smith."

"It's a *beautiful* night." He eased his way past her and stood on the doorstep. "I thought I'd take a walk along the beach, as far as the point—listen to the waves. Want to come?"

Stiffening, Capri stepped back a little. "I don't think so."

"You haven't been out all day, have you?" His brows lowered in a frown. "You know what they say: 'All work and no play make Jill a dull girl.'"

"Perhaps Jill wants to be a dull girl," she responded lightly. He was right, it *was* a beautiful night, with yellow stars pricking the purple sky and the air heady with disturbing perfumes that stirred her senses. A night made for romance...

"*Good night*, Mr. Smith."

"You don't know what you're missing." He grinned as he looped his thumbs under the heavy silver buckle of his belt, letting his long fingers splay down over his flat stomach. His fingernails were clean, square, neatly trimmed... "But tomorrow's another day," he murmured. "You haven't forgotten what I said about those termites, have you? I'll come over around ten. Okay?"

Capri suppressed a derisive snort. Did he really think she was going to sit at the kitchen table while he worked underfoot? No way. She'd make sure she was long gone by the time he arrived at ten...somewhere far from him, and his cocky self-assurance.

"Ten o'clock it is." She threw him a fake, saccharine-sweet smile and closed the door.

Leaning back against the rough wood, she listened till she heard his steps disappear, the smile gradually fading from her lips.

Why was it, she wondered, that this man who was everything she despised—lazy, arrogant, unambitious—attracted her so? That it was just a physical attraction didn't make her feel any better; if anything, it made her feel worse. Was she so unsophisticated that she could be drawn to a man just because of his body? By chemistry?

They had absolutely nothing in common.

She just couldn't understand how he could be satisfied to look after a few cabins for a living. And to look after them in such a lackadaisical fashion! He was very presentable-looking—oh, who did she think she was kidding; he would knock all the women dead if he appeared at a pool-side party in Houston?—and intelligent, if his quick tongue was anything to go by! He could surely do much better for himself than this mediocre job. Where was his pride—in himself, and his achievement?

With an impatient exclamation, Capri pushed herself away from the door. She really had much more important things to do than waste her time thinking about Taggart Smith!

Another perfect summer day!

Capri paused outside her cabin door at nine-thirty next morning, looking out at the ocean as she slung her red knapsack over her shoulder. The gently rippling water glittered under the rays of the sun, as if thousands of silver fish were skimming over the surface. The sheer beauty of it almost blinded her.

Against her will, she found her gaze drawn to the trees screening Taggart Smith's cabin. There was no sign of him . . .

Thank goodness! she told herself firmly. He was the very last person she wanted to see.

Leaving the door unlocked so that he could get in when he arrived at ten, Capri rounded the corner and began climbing up the gentle slope. In a couple of minutes she'd reached the top, and was within sight of the Walterses' cabin.

She approached it hesitantly. It wasn't that she was afraid the Walterses wouldn't be up yet—with an active toddler like Miranda the family would have been stirring a long time ago. It was just that Ellen might not accept her olive branch...

But she had barely knocked on the door when it opened and Ellen stood there, a welcoming smile on her face as she said, "Hi!"

Miranda appeared from behind her, her green eyes staring up unblinkingly as she wound her arms around one of her mother's legs.

"Hi." Capri's greeting included them both. "I...I was just passing, and I wondered——"

A man called out from somewhere inside the cabin. "Who's there, honey?"

Ellen's silver hoop earrings caught the light as she turned her head and called back, "It's the lady from cabin one, Sam——"

"Ask her to come in and join us for a cup of coffee."

An almost imperceptible frown marred Ellen's freckled brow as she turned toward the visitor standing on her doorstep, and Capri could almost read her thoughts—she had made advances once; was it safe to do so again?

"I'd *love* a cup of coffee." Capri put all the warmth she could into her tone; it wouldn't do to spurn another invitation. She stifled her impatience to get away to a quiet spot and start work.

"Oh, wonderful!" Ellen's smile was sunny as she pulled Capri inside. "Let's go through—we usually have our coffee in the kitchen, but we have company this morning."

Seconds before Ellen ushered her into the living room, Capri was struck by a strong feeling of foreboding. And when she saw the familiar blond figure sprawled lazily on an overstuffed love seat by the window she knew why.

She dragged her gaze from Taggart Smith's grinning, stubbled face as Ellen introduced her husband—a man as unlike Taggart as a man could be. He was short and compactly built, clean-shaven and with neatly trimmed dark hair that was beginning to recede at the temples.

The two men got up, and from the corner of her eye Capri could see Taggart watching her as she took the other man's outstretched hand and returned his firm grip.

"I'm Sam." Ellen's husband's voice was as warm as his brown eyes. "I'm pleased to meet you. And you're——?"

"She's Just Jones, Sam. Hi, Jones, how goes it this morning?"

Capri ignored Taggart's easy, teasing greeting. "My name's Capri," she said to Sam. "Capri Jones. I'm delighted to meet you."

Ellen had slipped from the room; now she came back with a steaming mug in her hand.

"You've already made Taggart's acquaintance?" Handing the coffee to Capri, she said, "Sugar or cream?"

Capri murmured, "Thanks, Ellen—no, I take it black."

With a gesture toward the love seat, Ellen added, "Do sit down."

Capri sank down onto the low-slung cushions, and felt her nerves tighten when Taggart dropped back to sit beside her. Inwardly cursing, she squished herself away from his large, muscled frame and pressed herself against the padded arm of the love seat. Immediately she heard

a deep chuckle...a chuckle which she ignored. "Yes,"
she said coolly, "Mr. Smith and I met yesterday."

"Capri." Taggart crossed his right leg over his left as
he murmured her name, and Capri noticed he wasn't
wearing socks under his Reeboks. Below the frayed hem
of his jeans, she could see a very nicely shaped tanned
ankle. "Let me guess..." He casually ran an arm along
the back of the seat. "Your parents were on holiday on
the Isle of Capri, and you were conceived there,
so—— "

"As a matter of fact," Capri turned a withering gaze
on him, "you are *partly* right. My parents *had* planned
a holiday there, but when my mother found out she was
pregnant she and my father decided they couldn't afford
the trip. So instead of a holiday, they got..."

Capri faltered momentarily. She was loath to tell him
that her mother had given birth to twins—that would
inevitably lead to questions about Jamie...questions that
even now she doubted she could answer without breaking
down.

"A baby!" Ellen's exclamation rescued her from her
dilemma.

Capri just smiled, and her hostess went on softly, "I'll
bet they were delighted." She had perched on the arm
of her husband's armchair, and now she caressed the
rounded bulge under her loose smock and addressed him.
"Babies beat fancy holidays any day, don't they,
Sammy?"

Sam slid his arm around her waist. "You can say that
again. There's nothing nicer than a baby."

"Baby!" Miranda looked up from the blocks she was
playing with and gave Taggart a dimpled smile. "Tiger.
Baby?"

"No, you precocious little miss!" Taggart laughed as
he leaned forward and rumpled her carroty curls. "I
don't have any babies!"

If Capri hadn't happened to glance at his face as
Miranda posed her artless question, she wouldn't have

noticed that his features had suddenly tautened. But because she did notice she was also very aware of his brief hesitation before he had answered.

Intriguing...

"No babies?" she said archly. "You're not a family man then?" The words were uttered before she had time to think. And once they were out, hanging in the air between them, she could do nothing but stare levelly at him and wait for his answer. When she saw his eyes shutter, saw his knuckles become ivory as his fingers tightened around his mug, she realized that Miranda had indeed touched a raw nerve.

"No," he said, shaking his head deliberately, "I'm not a family man."

Before Capri could come up with some snappy retort to lighten the moment, he said quietly, "And you? Are you the female equivalent—whatever it's called? A family woman?"

She sipped her coffee, wondering why she had started this conversation. Pushing to the back of her mind the ridiculous notion that she'd wanted to find out if there was a wife or fiancée in Taggart's life, she said, "No, I'm not. I'm a career woman. I have no intention of ever marrying."

Ellen looked at Capri, her green eyes puzzled. "I'm always surprised when I hear women say they don't want to get married. I know I'm old-fashioned, and my ideas seem to be out of touch with the present day... but," she shrugged helplessly, "I just couldn't imagine life without Sam, and Miranda—and this baby, of course, when it comes. My world would be so empty."

Sam got to his feet. Leaning over, he placed a warning hand on his wife's arm. "Honey, when people decide they'll never marry, they usually have a good reason."

A peach-colored flush swept up over Ellen's face. "Oh, Capri, I'm sorry. I just get on my soapbox and don't think before I speak—it's a bad habit of mine! Sam should put a piece of tape over my mouth——"

"Nonsense, Ellen." Taggart got to his feet now. "You only want everybody to be as happy as you and Sam, and there's nothing wrong with that. It's just that for some of us life isn't quite as simple as we'd like it to be." His mouth twisted in a reassuring smile, but Capri noticed it was a smile that didn't quite reach his eyes. "I have to go now, Ellen. Thanks for the coffee."

Capri purposefully avoided looking at him as he said, "See you later, Jones."

She wondered if he even heard her stiffly muttered, "Bye."

Sam followed him to the door, calling back to Ellen, "I'm going to take Miranda down to the beach for a walk."

"Righto, Sammy." Ellen sank down heavily into one of the armchairs with her mug of coffee.

Capri didn't relax till she heard the outside door slam shut behind them. Then, forcing her thoughts away from Taggart, she smiled and asked, "What does Sam do, Ellen?"

"Sammy? He's a sheet metal worker. He works in different places—travels over to Vancouver Island sometimes, and sometimes up the Sunshine Coast, sometimes to the interior. Eventually, he hopes to get a permanent job close to home."

"Are you lonely when he's away?"

Ellen laughed. "I don't have time to be lonely, Capri. I work too—I'm a secretary with one of the big forestry companies in downtown Vancouver. I have to get up at five-thirty every morning, and I rarely stop till around ten at night. By that time, I'm ready for bed...and when I put my head on the pillow, that's it till the alarm goes off next morning! I'm looking forward to having the baby—it'll be a rest! I plan to take a couple of months off after he—or she—arrives, then I'll be back on the job again."

"Who looks after Miranda?" Capri leaned forward. "A relative?"

Ellen shook her head. "The company I work for has on-site day care for its employees. Most day care places won't accept infants, so I consider myself very lucky. You see, Sam and I bought a house three years ago, and we'd never be able to afford the mortgage payments on one salary." She shrugged. "I have no choice but to work."

Capri felt a guilty flush tinge her cheeks. She was glad Ellen didn't know how wealthy she was... surely her money would create a gulf between them... Shifting uncomfortably on her seat, she slanted the topic of conversation in a different direction. "When's your baby due, Ellen?"

"Not for another month or so."

"You're not worried about being so far from the mainland... should things happen earlier?"

Ellen laughed. "No, I'm not worried. I went thirteen days past my due date with Miranda, and then it was a very long-drawn-out labor... the best part of two days! I'll probably be just as late this time... and have an equally long labor! We'll be going back home next week, though."

"You live in Vancouver?"

"North Vancouver. And you?"

"Houston, Texas."

Ellen looked frankly at her. "Sammy and I've been coming here for our holidays for years. You're the first person I've encountered who has come from so far away! What on earth made you pick Blueberry Island? Did you...?"

Her voice trailed away, and she bit her lip.

"What is it?" Capri raised her eyebrows, curious to know just why the other woman had paused. "You were going to say...?"

Ellen grimaced apologetically. "If Sammy were here, he'd be scolding me for being so nosy... but... it's just that there seemed to be something crackling in the air

between you and Taggart." She frowned. "Do you...
know him from somewhere?"

"Oh, *heavens*, no!" Capri drained the last of her
coffee, and placed the mug on the coffee-table. "He's
not the kind of man I——" She bit her lip, and her words
trailed away. She had been about to say, "He's not the
kind of man I associate with," but she'd realised in time
just how snobbish that would sound.

Ellen nodded knowingly. "He's not the kind of man
you're used to. I can tell."

"I'm not sure I know what you mean."

"It's not only the way you look—so elegant and
sophisticated—while Taggart's sort of...well, rough and
ready, I suppose you could call it. But you seem like two
totally different types...in your personalities. You're
reserved, and serious. Intense. Taggart's very laid-back
and very outgoing. The kind that makes friends easily.
He likes to have people around all the time." She sat
forward eagerly. "Has he asked you to his barbecue
tomorrow night?"

"Barbecue?"

"Oh, he obviously hasn't—yet. Don't worry, he's
going to. He's asking everyone on the island. It should
be a lot of fun..."

Don't worry, Ellen had said. That was the *last* thing
she would do, Capri thought—worry because Taggart
Smith hadn't invited her to a barbecue! Even if she received an invitation, she wouldn't accept it. At least she'd
know that tomorrow night she wouldn't have to be concerned about his popping unexpectedly into her life.

A short time later, after cheerily shouted goodbyes,
Capri began hiking along a cliff-top path on the western
side of the island, and as she did she waited for a rush
of satisfaction that at last she was going to have the
solitude she wanted.

But to her disappointment, it didn't come.

It didn't come then...and it still hadn't come by the
time she reached the end of the path and found herself

at the fringe of the forest. As she looked around aimlessly, she wondered why it was escaping her. This vacation spot was everything she'd expected...and more. It was beautiful, isolated, and quiet. What was wrong with her?

Oh, she knew only too well what was wrong! Taggart Smith was what was wrong. He was the fly in the ointment. If only he were caretaker on some other island. If only pigs had wings...

As she tossed down her knapsack, and settled on a dry, grassy spot under a strange gnarled tree with peeling red bark, she forced herself to think of something else...anything else. And as she drew out the files she had brought with her she remembered with exasperation that she'd forgotten that the purpose of her visit to the Walterses' cabin had been to invite Ellen for iced tea later on in the day. Taggart's presence had obliterated it from her mind.

There, she sighed helplessly, she was thinking about him again.

And as she did, Ellen's words slid insidiously back into her head...

"There seemed to be something crackling in the air between you and Taggart."

Of course, Capri grudgingly admitted, there *was* something crackling in the air between herself and the caretaker. Had he felt it too? But, even if *he* had, she hadn't thought it would be obvious to other people.

Anyway, whatever it was—some kind of electricity that was generated between them when they were together—it was something she had to defuse.

Involvement with Taggart Smith...or any other man...was the very last thing she wanted!

Capri returned to her cabin around four, to find that the caretaker had attended to the termite problem; a section had been neatly removed from the wall and replaced by another section of lighter wood.

And, to her surprise, someone had left a glass vase in the center of the table, a vase from which a charming bunch of floppy-headed blue wildflowers spilled abundantly. As she walked across the room to investigate, she noticed a note propped against the stem of the vase.

Slowly laying her knapsack on the floor, she frowned, despite her appreciation of the exquisite scent drifting from the blossoms. Who...?

She compressed her lips as she scanned the note. Taggart Smith's writing was like everything else about him—his scrawl was bold, his signature a lazily executed "T.S."

Island barbecue tomorrow six p.m., my place. Loud music will go on till dawn—best come, Jones; if you stay home, you'll not get a wink of sleep. Gone to mainland for provisions—back tomorrow afternoon.

Disgustedly she tossed the note down. Since when did caretakers throw parties for vacationing guests? Surely even in a casual setting like this island there should be some line drawn between staff and holidaymakers? Did Taggart Smith's employer know about—and approve of—his familiarity? And who was going to pay for the food...the hamburgers or steaks or whatever was going to be on the menu?

Well, she wasn't going to be any part of it! And she would tell him exactly that, when she got the opportunity——

All at once she realized she had plucked one of the blossoms from the vase, and had been staring at it, not really seeing it. Now she held it against her cheek, and the petals felt as smooth and light as the finest satin, the fragrance as sweet as a baby's breath. No one had ever given her wildflowers before—the caretaker's casual gesture touched her heart in a way that startled her.

With an abrupt little exclamation, she thrust the flower back into the vase. And, picking up his invitation, she tore it into a hundred pieces.

CHAPTER THREE

EARLY next morning, the sun beamed down on Capri as she cut through the water with strokes that were still crisp after an energetic half-hour swim. When she was about twenty feet from the jetty, in a shallow cordoned-off area, she rolled onto her back.

Lazily she floated, her long hair trailing on top of the water, her hands and feet weaving gently just under the surface as she caught her breath. Taggart Smith was over on the mainland; she could relax completely. Closing her eyelids to shut out the bright glare from the sky, she let her mind drift. Vaguely she was aware of the approaching sound of an outboard motor in the distance, the cry of a seagull close by, the sucking sound of the wavelets as they ran up the beach and then retreated again——

"Good morning, Jones! How's the water?"

She jerked her head around as the familiar, mocking voice carried clearly across the water. At first the sun blinded her, but when she saw Taggart Smith's tall figure uncoiling itself as he moored a large launch at the jetty she felt her heart give a great lurch.

It was just because she hadn't expected him to be back so early, she told herself—it had nothing whatsoever to do with the magnificence of his silhouetted frame.

As her eyes adjusted to the brightness, and she saw the keenly interested look he was bestowing on her, she cursed under her breath. What foul luck that she had chosen to put on her skimpiest bikini. It would undoubtedly provoke him into making a few lewd comments. The sooner she got rid of him, the better. And

43

the quickest way to do that was to make it quite clear that she wasn't interested in having a conversation with him.

"Good morning, Mr. Smith." Her tone was satisfyingly bored and unmistakably dismissive. "The water's warm."

She watched from under her long lashes as he tugged off his orange life jacket and tossed it down into the boat; next he unloaded a large red cooler and a bulky brown grocery bag, and as he stepped off the boat on to the jetty she blew out a sigh of relief. Good, he'd leave now.

But when she saw him peel off his T-shirt and kick off his running shoes, she frowned. What on earth...?

She stared disbelievingly as—jeans and all—he jumped into the water, the loud splash alarming into flight a sea gull that had been drifting nearby.

Was she seeing things?

No, she realized, she wasn't.

He began threshing straight for her, churning with his hands, kicking with his feet, in a comical—and quite astonishingly speedy—version of the doggy paddle.

Capri bit her teeth into her lower lip in an attempt to keep back an involuntary chuckle...but it bubbled out anyway. Didn't he know how ridiculous he looked, flailing around like that, with his teeth bared in a determined grimace, for all the world like a three-year-old learning to swim?

But as he reached her and thrust his upper body out of the water in a shower of spray just inches from where she was floating she felt her amusement dissipate abruptly. He looked so threateningly male, with his wet blond hair plastered close to his hard-boned head and the sun sparkling on his dripping shoulders, that she felt as if all the breath had been sucked from her lungs.

"Give me your hands," he ordered softly.

Without waiting for her co-operation, he pulled her up toward him, and her feet, in a flurry of movement, sought and found the sandy floor of the ocean. She swallowed some of the water that splashed into her face, and as she choked it out she looked up, gasping...

To find his gaze riveted on her near-naked figure.

Capri felt herself freeze. She had worn this particular bikini several times at Houston poolside parties without giving it a second thought. Now, in this remote and un-civilized situation, she suddenly realized just how out-rageously small were the three triangles of black adorning her curvy figure. She also realized she'd never in her life been so conscious of a man's appraisal.

Taggart's eyes had a glazed look, as if he'd been stunned by a falling tree.

Capri tried frantically to come up with some flippant remark to divert his attention, but before she could he shook his head, scattering droplets over her upturned face, and, shoving back the wet hair clamped to his brow, he brought his gaze to meet her own. The glazed look had disappeared as if it had never been, replaced now by an injured expression.

"You were laughing at me." His words held a gentle rebuke.

"Laughing at you?" Capri tried to pull herself from his grasp, but he adjusted his grip so that both of her wrists were captured in only one of his hands. She felt a tingling sensation sizzle up her arm and down to the pit of her stomach. "When was I laughing at you?"

"A minute ago. You were laughing at my swimming."

"No, really, I wasn't——"

"It's all right." With his free hand he plucked a small frond of seaweed from a spot just above her bikini top. Capri felt her breath catch in her throat as his fingertips trailed over her flesh a moment longer than was necess-ary. "You're not the first person who's laughed at me because I can't swim."

"You can't swim?" She ran a nervous tongue over her upper lip and tasted the salt of the ocean. "Didn't your parents enroll you in swimming lessons when you were a child?"

"My parents kicked me out of the house when I was eleven."

The words were spoken so matter-of-factly that at first Capri didn't take in what he'd said. Then she thought she must have been mistaken; nobody kicked out a child that age. But when she saw the bruised look shadowing his eyes she felt her heart clench. "Oh, Taggart..."

He didn't seem to notice that in her shocked distress she'd addressed him by his Christian name. "Sorry for me, Jones?" The question was asked in a steady tone.

Capri tried to answer, but couldn't. When *she* was eleven, her life had been golden...

She didn't shrink from Taggart when he released her wrists, she didn't push him away when he slid his hands around her waist. How could she, when he'd been so rejected already, in his young life?

But when he pulled her body abruptly toward him and she felt her wet flesh against his she drew in her breath with a sharp sound of protest. The current sizzling between them was like nothing she had ever experienced before.

"Kind of dangerous," he murmured, "to be standing in water with so much electricity around."

So he felt it too! But how could he not? Capri wondered, her head spinning. "Then we must either turn it off, or else get out of the water." Her voice was shaky.

"We're safe so long as we're touching." He pulled her even closer, and Capri felt the water swirling around her hips.

She knew he was going to kiss her...and she knew that if she wanted to stop him now was the time. But instead of wrenching herself away from him she found herself digging her toes deeper into the sand as he lowered his head toward her.

His lips were firm and demanding, and they tasted of salt and sun, and something else, something that was his own. She had never been kissed before by a man with a beard—even one with only a few days' growth—and she'd never realized what she'd missed. It added a new dimension, a tickly and altogether intoxicating dimension, to a kiss that even without the beard would have made her feel as tipsy as if she'd been drinking champagne!

Her hands had somehow found their way to his shoulders, and her fingers were caressing the smooth skin stretched tautly over his hard, corded muscles. She forced her thoughts away from the delicious shivers that were spiraling through her, focused them instead on the sympathy she felt for him—the sympathy which, she reminded herself sturdily, was the only reason she was in his embrace.

No wonder he'd looked so somber when he'd said he wasn't a family man. With his wretched background, why would family life appeal to him?

With a moan of compassion, she returned his kiss, wanting to let him know, without words, that she felt for him because of the cruelty he'd suffered as a child. She tried to ignore the way her body was reacting to the caress of his hands on her water-slicked back, and the rasping of his wet jeans against her naked midriff. She didn't want this to be a sexual experience, she wanted it to be a sharing, a comforting...

She twined her fingers together at his nape, and with a sigh let her body melt against his, parting her lips, inviting him to enjoy what she was offering so generously——

With a suddenness that made her gasp, he pulled away from her, untwining the hands she had so tightly clasped round his neck.

She stood for a moment, eyes shut, unwilling to believe what had happened. When she blinked her lids open, she saw, to her bewilderment, that Taggart was looking down at her with an amused expression that was totally incompatible with the intimacy they'd just shared...

His smile, Capri noted in a distant part of her mind, would have been Hollywood-perfect had it not been for a tiny chip at the corner of one of his teeth——

"It works every time." He slid his thumbs lazily into the waistband of his sodden jeans.

Capri stared. What on earth did he mean? What worked every time?

He must have seen the question in her eyes, but instead of giving an answer he just chuckled. Then, turning away, with the neatest dive she'd ever seen he sliced into the water.

Capri watched, openmouthed, utterly disbelieving, as he pulled toward the jetty in a crawl so powerful, so fast, and so flawless that he could have been an Olympic swimmer.

A couple of minutes later, he was striding up the beach with the red cooler under one arm, the bulky brown grocery bag under the other.

Just before he reached the trees sheltering his cabin, he paused and looked back to where Capri was still standing waist-deep in the water, arms clutched around herself, cold wet hair straggling like rats' tails over her shoulders.

"Oh, by the way, Jones——" His shout was loud and cheerful. "I almost forgot. See you tonight...at the barbecue! Great food...and even greater music! The first tape I put on will be just for you."

Capri didn't answer. She *couldn't* answer. She couldn't even move.

But if she *could* have moved, and if she'd had a gun, she would have shot him.

She had sometimes wondered, idly, if she had it in her to kill someone.

Her teeth began to chatter. After what Taggart Smith had just done to her, she knew she'd never need to ask herself that question again.

She stayed in her cabin for the rest of the day, leaving it only when she had to use the outhouse. On one such occasion, around eleven o'clock, as she'd opened her kitchen door she'd seen Taggart going over the top of the hill in the direction of the Walterses' cabin. Not wanting him to notice her, she had hung back till he was out of sight.

He was probably going to regale them with the story of how she'd made such a fool of herself...as, of course, she had. She just couldn't believe she'd let herself be taken in that way. No wonder he'd laughed at her...and was probably still laughing at her.

And, despite his "See you tonight" he must know darned well she wouldn't turn up at his barbecue...not after the way he'd humiliated her.

At around a quarter to six, she switched off her computer. She had achieved very little, she admitted frustratedly, other than transferring some of the statistics from the files to one of her floppy disks. Her thoughts had kept veering away from the report, kept veering back to Taggart's kiss, to the heat that had filled her body as his lips had moved persuasively on hers——

Abruptly she tugged open the fridge door and took out the ingredients for a green salad. A few minutes later, as she was taking an unappetizing can of tuna from the cupboard, suddenly, tantalizingly, the smell of steaks sizzling on a barbecue came drifting through her open window.

"No," she muttered, "forget it. I'm *not* going to his barbecue!"

But as she jerked her head from side to side in adamant denial stereo music started. The beat drummed languidly into the evening air—and through the trees, across the long grass, and into the small kitchen came the full, rich sound of Brenda Lee's voice, crooning out the lyrics from one of Capri's all-time favorite songs, "I'm Sorry."

She smiled, despite herself. She could just picture the caretaker's blue eyes twinkling with amusement as he had chosen the tape and put it on.

Slowly, like snow melting under a warm April shower, all her hostility disappeared. She even chuckled. Oh, come on, she admitted, what had happened that morning had really been very funny—where had her sense of humor gone! She'd spoiled a perfectly lovely day by sulking indoors, feeling angry—and achieving nothing. If she stayed home now she *knew* she'd not get any work done. Was she going to waste the evening too?

She found herself humming along with the music as she covered the salad bowl with plastic wrap and put the can of tuna back in the cupboard. Who knew? She might even enjoy herself!

For, despite the social chasm that existed between herself and the caretaker, she couldn't deny that things were never dull when he was around. He had a style all his own, a style that was, undoubtedly, laid-back—but, after all, this was Lotus Land...wasn't that how Bill at Spartan's Lo-Cost Holidays had described the West Coast? She, not Taggart Smith, was the one who was out of step!

What should she wear? Standing in front of her open closet, she surveyed her selection of clothes indecisively. Finally, she slid a pair of ice-blue Levi's from their hanger, and from the shelf a matching long-sleeved cotton sweater with her initials embroidered in silver on the breast pocket. After a moment's hesitation, she added her pile-lined navy blue windbreaker; it was still warm outside, but it might cool off after dark. And hadn't Taggart intimated that the music would go on till dawn?

Ten minutes later, as she carefully applied a coat of fuchsia lipstick, she realized she was shivering. She paused, and stared bewilderedly at her reflection in the mirror.

Why was it that she never felt this breathless excitement—never saw that sparkle in her gray-green eyes or that natural flush in her cheeks—when she was getting ready for the glitzy parties she occasionally attended in Houston?

Did it have anything to do with the kiss she'd shared with Taggart Smith that morning? She saw her color deepen as she recalled how, several times during the day, she'd asked herself how far she would have gone with him if he hadn't pulled away. Shying away from the question, she'd felt tingling sensations quivering through her body... just as they were doing now.

With a frustrated exclamation, she stuffed the lipstick back into her makeup bag. Her train of thought was ridiculous. She found Taggart Smith physically attractive—what was the point in denying it? But to consider for even a moment that she might have let him make love to her in the fullest sense was insane.

And insane she was not.

Capri walked through the long grass, enjoying the music drifting through the still evening air.

Taggart had played a number of Brenda Lee songs after "I'm Sorry"; now the voice of Placido Domingo mingled exquisitely with that of Maureen McGovern as together they sang "A Love Until the End of Time."

Capri had a tape of the duet at home, and listened to it often. Invariably it left her with a vague yearning somewhere deep in her soul, but never had its haunting perfection affected her the way it was doing tonight...

She paused for a moment in the shadows as she reached the trees, closing her eyes as the voices finally faded away. This little island was beginning to weave a strange spell around her...

Shaking her head to dislodge the unwelcome thought, she stepped out briskly along the path leading to the cabin.

Taggart had set out patio chairs and loungers, and Sam and several other people were sitting around a large cedar table. Ellen was over by the barbecue...with Taggart.

Capri felt every nerve in her body leap to life as her gaze flicked over him. She had never seen a man so incredibly good-looking...nor one who wore his looks so casually, as if he wasn't even aware of them. Tonight his shoulders looked broader than ever under a big denim shirt that hung loosely over his tight-fitting jeans, the shirt unbuttoned, the sleeves rolled halfway up his forearms. He was expertly wielding a pair of tongs over the barbecue...

Capri frowned. He looked different from the way he had that morning—was it because most of his blond hair was hidden by the white chef's hat cocked so jauntily on his head? She felt a strange tugging at her throat when he looked up—no, that wasn't it. He had shaved! She had guessed at the strength of the jaw under his blond stubble, but what her imagination hadn't provided was the attractive vertical dimple clefting his chin.

Her heart did a crazy flip-flop as he caught her eye and smiled his lazy smile.

"Hey, Jones, glad you decided to come..."

Some of the others turned around and Capri called, "Hi," lightly as she walked past them and approached the barbecue. "Something smells good!" She glanced at her host only briefly as she spoke to him, then, tossing her jacket on the back of a chair, she addressed Ellen.

"Where's your bundle of mischief? Don't tell me there's a baby-sitting service on Blueberry Island!"

Ellen gestured toward Taggart with the celery stick she'd been nibbling on. "You're looking at it," she chuckled. "Miranda was cranky when Sam and I brought her here—she didn't have a proper nap this afternoon—so Taggart took her off our hands. He pulled out his camp-bed in the living room and tucked her in there with her teddy; she went out like a light. I've never seen her settle so quickly!" She grinned up at Taggart. "You have a wonderful way with children!"

Indeed he did have a wonderful way... and not only with children! Capri felt herself flush as she recalled how she'd surrendered to his caresses that morning——

"Ellen, come here a minute, honey." Sam's voice called out from the other group, and with an apologetic grimace and a murmured, "Excuse me" Ellen moved away to join her husband.

Capri fought a cowardly urge to follow the redhead. Taggart's eyes were twinkling smugly as he looked down at her, and she knew only too well that he was remembering what had happened between them in the water. She felt her senses tingle, just as they had tingled then, and in a desperate effort to fight her reaction to him she said the first thing that came into her head.

"Such a waste, Mr. Smith, to have a wonderful way with children, in view of the fact that you don't have any of your own."

As soon as she'd spoken, Capri regretted the words. She had seen how upset he'd been at Ellen's when she'd asked him if he was a family man, so why was she needling him? Was she trying to pay him back for the way he'd tricked her into kissing him? Hadn't she already decided he'd just been having a bit of harmless fun?

"Yes," Taggart appeared to be concentrating on what he was doing as he flipped a steak over, "it *is* a waste."

"You want to have children, then?"

"Let's just say I've...considered the possibility."

His voice was taut and Capri felt a twinge of guilt. But what she had started, she decided, she should have the courage to finish. "I suppose you feel that your life-style wouldn't be the best for bringing up a family."

The steak sizzled as he added a dollop of some red-brown sauce from a small jar and spread it over the surface with a brush. "My life-style?" His eyes were hooded as he looked down at her.

Capri glanced around her with a derisive expression. "Well, it is rather primitive here—I don't see any schools, hospitals, stores... This remote island may suit a single man, but as a permanent residence for a couple with a family——"

"Ah, I see. So if you and I, for example, were to get married," his tone was mocking, "you'd want things to change. You'd want *me* to change——"

"You and I, thank heavens, will never have to face up to that problem—at least, not together! But yes, of course I'd expect you to change. People do, you know. A friend of mine who swore her career came before anything changed her mind almost overnight when she fell in love. Now she's married, and she's given up her very successful job in real estate to stay home with her baby. Of course, she had to make a big sacrifice..."

Taggart's mouth twisted into a mirthless smile. "I know people change their life-styles, and it wouldn't be impossible for me to change mine. But," he drawled, "the whole question's academic, because to have children I'd first have to find me a woman who would make the kind of sacrifice you're talking about worthwhile, and..." With an eloquent shrug of his shoulders, he let his words trail away.

Capri wondered, bewilderedly, why she felt as if he'd poured a bucket of cold water over her. Was it because she was taking his comment personally? She felt as if he'd lumped her in with all the other women he knew, none of whom reached the standard he was looking for in a wife. It made her feel as if she was lacking in some way. But why on earth would she care? What did it matter to her if some laid-back Canadian caretaker didn't consider her good enough for him? "You seem to think very highly of yourself, Mr. Smith——"

"Leave it, Jones." His voice was so grim that Capri felt a little shiver run through her. But before she could try to figure out exactly what she'd said to provoke such an intense response he thrust the tongs into her hand. "Here, keep an eye on the steaks and I'll get you a drink. Beer or wine?"

"A glass of wine, please." Capri's words were mechanically uttered. His abrupt change of subject had thrown her...but only for a moment. It had been swiftly swept from her mind as his fingers had brushed against hers when she took the tongs. Once again, she found herself shivering—as she seemed to do every time they touched.

Why was it, she wondered, that when she was around Taggart Smith she had less control over herself than a lemming bound disastrously for the sea...?

She blinked back to awareness as a hand passed in front of her eyes.

"This is supposed to be a party, Jones, not a séance."

Capri felt a rush of color flare in her cheeks. Had her expression given away any of her thoughts? She hoped not! "Sorry," she said, "I was dreaming..."

Taggart took the tongs from her and gave her a tulip-shaped plastic glass three-quarters filled with a sparkling pink wine.

"I suppose writers are permitted to do that—slip in and out of their imaginary worlds when the muse takes them. So," he said teasingly, "how's the story coming? Is the fly still in the ointment?"

Capri sipped her wine, then looked up at him over the rim of the glass. "The fly's still there, but somehow," she said ruefully, "I seem to be getting used to him. By the way, thank you for the flowers. I assume you left them——"

"Mm. Strangely, they made me think of you, though I'm sure you're used to something more sophisticated."

"They're lovely. But you're right," she said lightly, "in the city, men seem more disposed to present a woman with a bouquet of perfect red roses, or——"

"Damn!"

Capri blinked as Taggart's abrupt oath ripped into the air.

"You're distracting me, Jones!" Moving so fast his actions were little more than a blur, he removed the steaks one by one from their position on the rack above the white-hot coals and transferred them to a large tin platter. "Almost burned them! Now," his tone was apologetic, "fascinating though our conversation was becoming, I'm afraid it will have to wait." He flashed her a quick smile and said, "We'll talk later, okay?"

"Oh...sure..."

As if he'd already forgotten all about her, Taggart called out, "Hey, everyone, time to eat. Come and help yourself to a plate. Ellen, would you mind going inside and fetching the salads and dressings from the fridge? Jones, you can help...the rolls are in the oven."

Capri realized that her comment about the roses had probably sounded snobbish; she hadn't meant it that way. Had Taggart not interrupted her, she had been going to say she much preferred the exquisitely lovely wildflowers...

She laid her wineglass on the edge of a small table by the barbecue, and followed Ellen into the cabin. The moment had passed. It was too late. But as she tumbled the rolls from the hot tray into a round basket on the countertop she found her gaze drawn irresistibly out the window to where Taggart was standing. He must have sensed someone's eyes on him, because he turned his head toward the cabin inquiringly. When he saw Capri, he winked and threw her a friendly grin.

Capri turned away, her breath coming out in a trembling sigh. What a *fool* she had been to come to the barbecue. From the very first moment she'd set eyes on Taggart Smith, she'd found him physically attractive. But she had never anticipated that it would be a problem . . . after all, she had felt nothing but contempt for him! But that had changed. When it had happened, or where, she didn't quite know, but it had. She was, she realized with dismay, growing to like the man.

She pressed her lips together as she took the basket of warm rolls and made for the door. She would have to make sure she kept her distance from him, for liking him was a complication.

A complication, she decided irritably, that she could well do without!

Plate heaped high with steak, baked potato, a variety of salads and a buttered roll, Capri made her way with Ellen to the chairs arranged around the cedar table. A few minutes later, everyone else had taken their seats...except Taggart, who was still over by the barbecue.

"Have you met these guys, Capri?" Sam waved his beer glass towards the assorted group.

"No." She smiled. "I haven't."

"Ah, let me do the honors, then . . ."

Capri shook hands in turn with Gord, Mike, Graham, and Judd, four university rugby players who shared a cabin at the north end of the island, and then with a wiry bald-headed man called Paul, and his plump gray-haired wife, Joanna.

"Ellen tells me you come from Houston, dear." Joanna speared a cherry tomato and popped it whole into her mouth. After chewing for a moment, she went on, "How are you enjoying the island?"

"Very much, thanks."

"Good." Joanna sipped from her glass of beer, leaving a trace of froth on her upper lip. "Paul and I have been coming here for years—we wouldn't dream of going anywhere else for our holidays. Gord, you must get Paul to tell you about the students who were in your cabin last year. They were more fun than a barrel of monkeys..."

As Joanna prattled gaily on, Capri found her attention drawn inexorably back to Taggart. He had just placed a baked potato on his plate beside his steak, and as she peeked from beneath her long lashes she saw him carefully add sour cream, green onions, and bacon bits, his brow drawn down in concentration as he did.

She couldn't drag her gaze away, despite the almost painful tugging of her heartstrings as she watched him. Oh, she knew what caused the gnawing ache—no point in pretending she didn't. Beauty always affected her that way. And Taggart Smith *was* beautiful, in a totally masculine way. From the tousled strands of blond hair which had slipped from under his chef's hat to the tips of his Reeboks he was utterly, undeniably magnificent. Why, then, did she not feel uplifted by such a splendid sight? Why did she feel this vague, unfocused yearning, somewhere deep inside her soul? As if looking at him wasn't quite enough? As if——

"Sorry I'm late..."

Capri's thoughts scattered as a young woman appeared around the corner of the cabin—a very striking young woman, with long blond hair fashioned in a thick braid that hung down her back, almost to her waist. She was wearing a tight-fitting black sweater which accentuated the aggressive thrust of her breasts, and white stretch pants which rippled like a second skin over her rounded buttocks and long shapely legs as she sauntered across to the barbecue.

Fixing her brown eyes possessively on Taggart, she ignored everyone else. "Pour me a beer, Tag," her lips curved in a sultry smile, "and I'll cook my own steak."

Capri watched, hypnotized, as the latecomer whisked off the chef's hat and perched it atop her own head. Then, sliding an arm around Taggart's waist, she planted a lingering kiss on his jaw.

A mixture of strange emotions surged through Capri, some of which she couldn't identify. One she could, and that was anger. When Taggart had been fooling around with her in the water that morning, had this blonde been waiting for him? Had he gone straight from one to the other? Did she live in his cabin with him? What was the relationship between them?

She bent toward Ellen, and, trying to sound nonchalant, murmured, "Who's the new arrival?"

"Why, that's Zoe." Ellen turned and looked at Capri. "Haven't you met her yet? Oh, no, I guess not—she had a couple of days off... she was away before you arrived, and just got back from the mainland late this afternoon." She chuckled. "She's quite something, isn't she? Not your run-of-the-mill caretaker!"

Capri felt as though someone had removed her brain. She stared at Ellen. "Caretaker? What do you mean? She's a caretaker? Surely a setup this size doesn't need *two* of them?"

"Two of them?" Now it was Ellen's turn to be puzzled. "There's only one—Zoe."

"But... but what about Taggart? Isn't he...?"

Capri's words trailed away as she saw the incredulous expression on Ellen's face. "Taggart?" Her laugh was a low gurgle. "You thought Taggart was a *caretaker*?"

"He isn't...?" The other woman shook her head, and Capri swallowed disbelievingly. Then she answered her own question... "He isn't," she said in a flat tone. After Ellen's giggles dissipated, Capri went on quietly, "If he's

not the caretaker of the Blueberry Cove Cabins, then
who is he?''

Ellen took a tissue from the pocket of her smock, and
wiped the tears from her eyes. "Oh, Capri, I thought
you knew.

"Taggart Smith owns the island.''

CHAPTER FOUR

"HE OWNS the island?"

Capri couldn't have felt more shocked if she'd been told Taggart Smith was a Russian spy.

Surely Ellen must be mistaken?

But suddenly a memory flickered in her brain... the memory of Taggart's self-assured bearing as he had approached her cabin door the afternoon of her arrival. Only too clearly she recalled her own irritation—and her thoughts—as she'd surveyed his arrogant swagger... he walked as if he owned the very ground over which he strode.

"But the boy who took me over in his boat pointed this out as the caretaker's cabin..."

Capri hadn't realized she'd whispered her thoughts aloud, till she heard Ellen's voice murmuring a response.

"Everyone refers to this as the caretaker's cabin, honey—and most of the time it is. But it's the one where Taggart keeps his things, and when he comes to the island he likes to use it. It has the most convenient location. Zoe uses it when he's not here, and she moves temporarily to another one, up by the woods, when he is. He's never here for more than a week or so, at most."

A dull headache throbbed to life and Capri pressed a hand against her temple in a vain attempt to subdue it.

What a *fool* she'd been.

But if *she* had been a fool, Taggart Smith had been a deceitful, despicable b——

A firm hand on her shoulder made her jump. Swiveling round, she found him standing behind her, the sun glinting in his hair so that the fine strands looked like spun gold. "Was somebody talking about me?" he murmured innocently. "I could have sworn I heard my name mentioned . . ."

Capri knew by his tone that he had heard not only his name. He had heard *everything* that had been said . . . and he knew she was now aware of his little deception.

If he had looked in the least remorseful or apologetic, she might have been able to rein in her anger. But when she saw the way his perfect lips were twitching, saw the unholy twinkle in his beautiful blue eyes, something snapped inside her.

Wrenching her shoulder from his warm grasp, she pushed back her chair and got to her feet. "I'm leaving, Mr. Smith." She wished futilely that he wasn't so tall; her attempt to look down her nose at him failed miserably. "I should never have come."

She sensed that Ellen was staring at her; was aware that Sam also had turned toward her. She ignored them. She ignored them all. The music had stopped—as had the hubbub of conversation. The only sound as she snatched up her jacket and departed self-righteously along the path was the flip-flop of her sandals on the sun-baked sand.

Once past the trees, out of sight of the others, she found her pace slowing, found the first flare of her anger subsiding just a little. Instead of heading for her cabin, she walked down to the end of the jetty, where she stood staring out at the silver-blue rippling waters.

Her throat tightened. What had set out to be a perfect vacation was fast becoming a total disaster. And all because of Taggart Smith.

The ache at her temples throbbed to a crescendo, and wearily she tried to erase it with her palms. "What a rotten thing to do," she whispered, her view suddenly blurred. "Rotten. Just rotten."

"You're right, Jones. It *was* rotten."

Capri froze. For a moment, she thought the sound must have been the murmur of the waves, but in her heart she knew it wasn't. It was Taggart. If she hadn't been so consumed by her own tangled emotions she'd surely have heard his firm tread behind her on the weathered wooden planks.

"Look at me, Jones," he ordered softly.

She shook her head, not wanting him to see the shine of her tears. "Go away. Leave me alone."

She stiffened as she felt his fingers curve relentlessly around her shoulders, but despite her attempt to shrug off his grip he turned her to face him.

"Does it make a difference?" he asked quietly.

"Difference?" Capri knew exactly what he meant, but she shook her head, pretending bewilderment.

He took one of her slender hands in his. "Something's been happening between us." His voice had a husky timbre. "You've been fighting it, shying away from it. If you had known I wasn't the caretaker, would it have made a difference?" He caressed the sensitive skin at her wrist with the pad of his thumb as he spoke, sending little shivers through Capri.

"Of course not! Your job has nothing to do with——" She broke off abruptly, realizing she was giving too much away.

"Go on."

To her dismay, Capri felt a slow curling heat spark to life inside her as he continued to tease her skin with his thumb. She tilted her chin defiantly. "Why should it?"

"Because as a rule people of your type don't socialize with caretakers——"

"People of my type?" Capri interrupted coldly. "Would you mind being a bit more explicit?"

"It's hard to be explicit . . . it's difficult to define. But you have a certain look—and a certain attitude—that can't be bought. An aura, if you will, that spells——" Taggart shrugged "—breeding and old money. It has to do with the fine, aristocratic structure of your bones, the regal tilt of your head, the graceful way you walk...even the way you wear your clothes.''

Capri was well aware of what he was talking about—her parents had both been from wealthy old Boston families and he had come pretty close to describing them, and the people with whom they had mixed—but she kept her expression blank as she met Taggart's shrewd gaze. "I'm wearing what anyone else would wear to a barbecue, Mr. Smith. A little cotton sweater and a pair of Levi's——"

"What I'm talking about has nothing to do with clothes per se, though I imagine that pretty little sweater has an impressive designer label hand-sewn inside the neckline, and probably cost more than Ellen Walters earns in a week." He shook his head. "You're a mystery, Jones. If I may quote an old line, 'What's someone like you doing in a place like this?' Why aren't you holidaying on the Riviera, or——?"

"For a man who appears to be so smart, you have a remarkably short memory," Capri retorted. "I told you why I'm here on the day I arrived. I have work to do, and this little island *seemed* to promise me peace and quiet. I don't give a damn whether you're the caretaker or the king of——"

Her words were choked off as Taggart looped his arms around her and trapped her, pulling her so close her breasts were pressed against his ribs. "If you really don't give a damn," he murmured, "then why have you been so standoffish with me?"

"Good grief, but you're conceited!" Capri was forced to look up at him—the only other option was to let her face be pressed into the crisp hairs curling at the open neck of his shirt where she would surely suffocate in the heady scent of his skin! "Surely you don't expect that *every* woman who crosses your path is going to want to tumble into bed with you?"

Capri felt the vibration of his deep chuckle against her ribs. "A man can always dream... No, Jones, but when the chemistry between two people is as explosive as it is between the two of us we'd have to be crazy to ignore it—and *I'm* not crazy... are you?"

"I think I've got to be!" Capri snapped. "To be standing here like this—with a man who's virtually a stranger—talking... about..." She lost her train of thought as he slid one hand to her nape, weaving his fingers through her hair.

"We don't have to remain strangers," he said silkily. "I don't want that...and I think that deep down neither do you. Since we just argue when we talk, why don't we try another route to getting to know each other?"

In a move that stunned her with its unexpectedness, he slid his left hand down to settle firmly over her rear end, the fingers splayed out possessively as he drew her lower body so close to his that she could feel his hard heat through the fabric of her jeans.

She jerked out a protest, but his mouth closed over her parted lips in a masterful, sensual kiss that took her breath away and sent erotic little shivers dancing right to the tips of her toes. Dazzled by sheer sensation, she was aware of nothing but the persuasive movement of his firm warm flesh on her own... and the male scent of him, the sweet heady taste of him, the smoothness of his closely shaven jaw against her even smoother skin. The kiss seemed to go on for ever, drawing her, beguiling her...

Bewitching her, so that she hardly noticed that he had slid his tongue between her lips. Only when it started to tangle with hers in an erotic mating did she gasp with dismay and wrench her mouth away.

"Let me go..." Desperately, she tried to conceal how intensely affected she was by his aggressive, seductive kissing. "If you do," she bargained breathlessly, "I'll tell you why I was standoffish——"

"You will?" he murmured, sliding his lips along her jawbone in a caress that provoked a squirm of pleasure.

"I will." She tried not to dwell on the quivering response she felt as his lips brushed the skin under her ear. "It was because I believed that as a caretaker—on a scale of one to ten, I thought you rated a zero! It had nothing to do with you as a person."

His attention had moved to her ear, and now he paused only long enough in his delicate nibbling of the sensitive shell-pink lobe to ask, "And on a scale of one to ten, as someone who only *pretended* to be a caretaker, how would I rate?" before resuming his tender torture.

Capri stifled a despairing groan. "Probably around a..." she tried without success to keep her voice from trembling, "a five or a s..." Her words trailed away in a feeble squeak. His lips had prowled from her earlobe to her neck and by some freaky chance had hit on a spot that was excruciatingly and exquisitely sensitive. She felt a deep shudder rake through her. No, she thought weakly, not a five, or even a six...much more likely a nine. She whimpered as his foraging lips concentrated on nerve-endings she hadn't known existed. Or possibly even a ten! "For the love of Pete," she pleaded, "will you stop *doing* that? You promised you'd let me go!"

"Did I? First tell me if you agree with me——"

"About what?"

"About this thing that's happening between us."

Why deny it? It would only make it seem more important than it was. "I agree with you," she choked out grudgingly. "There's a certain...chemistry between us, but——"

"But what, Jones?"

Capri gasped to fill her lungs with air. "It's just lust, Mr. Smith," she retorted breathlessly, "and——"

"And what's wrong with lust? Why deny our sensuous appetite? We're adults——"

"Lust is animal desire...and we're not animals—at least, I can't speak for you, but *I* don't consider myself an——"

'Hey, Tag!'

The shouted interruption made Capri start. Panting a little, she wriggled free as Taggart's grip loosened, and she turned her head. There, standing at the edge of the trees, was Zoe.

How long had she been there?

Capri darted a glance at Taggart, but she couldn't tell from his expression whether or not he was concerned that they might have been observed.

"Come on, Tag," Zoe's tone was impatient, "I need you."

Taggart waved and—voice slightly husky—called back, "Be right there!"

The easy rapport between them was unmistakable. Capri, hugging her arms around herself, frowned as she felt a dart of hostility toward Zoe. Why on earth should she feel that way toward a woman she didn't even know?

"Come with me, Jones." Taggart's voice was low, warm and inviting.

Capri shook her head as she watched the young blond woman saunter away to disappear beyond the trees.

His gaze narrowed. "You're still mad at me."

Capri almost said, "No." And it would have been the truth. But it would make it easier to get rid of him if she pretended she was. "Yes," she replied, stabbing him with a sharp glance, "I am. I don't like fakes."

"Ah, but you're one too, aren't you?"

"Of course I'm not!" But even as she spoke Capri realized what he was referring to. "Oh..." She uttered a frustrated exclamation.

His eyebrows quirked sardonically. "You're no writer, are you? You're far too sensible, too practical, to write romances. They're full of emotion, Jones. And that is a quality which you seem to be sadly lacking. Oh, I admit you appeared to show a tiny spark of warmth this morning in the water, but I could sense you were kissing me out of a sense of...duty. With maybe a smidgeon of guilt thrown in. No, if you have any real honest-to-goodness emotion inside you, it's so tightly under control that it might as well not exist. A pity. You're a stunningly beautiful woman, but——'' he shrugged ''—so is Venus de Milo, and though she's wonderful to look at a man wants something more than a statue when he——''

''Oh, but I'm not like Venus de Milo——''

''You're not?'' He cocked a hopeful eyebrow at her. ''Now that's what I wanted to hear——''

Capri's hand blurred past her eyes as it sliced to Taggart's cheek, the sound of her slap like an insult to the sweet evening air...the impact stinging on her flesh. She wasn't about to let him, or anyone else, compare her to a lifeless image! ''In case you hadn't noticed,'' she said in an icy tone, ''*I* have arms!''

She had acted impulsively, with no thoughts of his reaction, but now she braced herself, waiting for the anger she was sure must follow.

To her amazement, she saw a rueful smile crease his face. ''Well, well, well! You pack quite a punch when you're angry. Now if only you could be as free and easy with your other emotions! They've got to be in there somewhere; it's too bad they're frozen——''

''Oh, what a typically arrogant male attitude!'' Capri blazed. ''You think that if a woman turns you down it must be because there's something wrong with *her*! There's nothing wrong with me, Mr. Smith. I'm just not interested in having sex with you——''

''It would be fun.'' Again his eyes caressed her with the smoothness of blue velvet.

''Fun?'' Capri echoed scathingly. ''*Fun?* And what about afterward?''

''What about afterward?'' His expression had become wary.

"How would we feel afterward? Something that starts out as . . . 'fun' . . . can turn into something quite different. And someone might get hurt."

"Then we'd have to face that when it happened, wouldn't we?"

"I'm sorry," she said stiffly. "I'm not prepared to take that risk."

"That's what I figured." He reached out and grazed her cheek with the back of his right hand. "I'd lay ten to one someone has hurt you in the past . . . and whoever he was he did a damn good job. I'm sorry." His tone was gentle. "But if you should change your mind you know where my cabin is—even if you just want to talk. Any time of the day or night . . ."

Capri had jerked away from him, but not quickly enough, and as he strode away along the jetty she felt her skin tingling where he'd touched.

She watched him till she couldn't see him any longer. Her anger, she realized, had flared and died again as quickly as if it had never been. Somewhere deep inside her instead she felt an ache . . . a yearning to call out to him, to tell him to wait . . . that she'd changed her mind.

But she didn't.

And as she began trudging unhappily toward her cabin she was almost overcome by feelings of futile regret. It was as if something of great value had been within her grasp, and she had foolishly let it slip away.

Capri closed the door of the outhouse behind her and stepped out into the moonlit night. Carefully gathering the folds of her ivory silk nightshirt around her to protect it from the thorny branches edging the narrow path, she made her way back along the path to her cabin.

She had gone to bed around one, shortly after the party had ended and the music had stopped, but she'd been unable to sleep. Around three, she'd finally realized that one of the reasons for her sleeplessness was hunger.

Getting up, she'd lit her lamp and made herself a bacon sandwich and a mug of hot chocolate. Then before turning in again she'd decided she'd better pay a last visit to the outhouse.

Now with a restless sigh, she walked along the side of her cabin. The night air was heavy with the scent of wildflowers and the tang of the sea . . . and with the lingering aroma of the bacon she'd fried——

The huge dark shape outlined in the light washing from her open doorway took Capri by complete surprise as she turned the corner. For a moment she hesitated disbelievingly, putting a hand against the wall to support herself as she stared with blank eyes. What could it be? A shadow? An optical illusion? A . . .?

Her heart stopped. No shadow. No illusion.

A bear. An enormous black bear.

It stood on its hind legs, pawing the air in front of it, beady eyes shining at her like two tiny glittering laser beams——

She tried to scream but couldn't. Every muscle in her throat had tightened so that no air, no sound could pass through it. The only scream she was capable of was the silent scream of terror that started somewhere deep in the darkest part of her soul and, with a speed that left her shaking, swelled to an unbearable pitch and threatened to explode inside her.

Run! urged every cell in her body. Run!

Adrenalin coursed through her, giving her the impetus she needed. Turning on her heels, she raced blindly away from the cabin—away from the hideous, sour-smelling creature that had appeared out of nowhere.

She stumbled as one of her sandals caught on something and fell off, but she just kicked off the other and kept running, hardly aware of the sharp pain against her soles as she stepped on sharp rocks hidden in the long grass. Her lungs were bursting with pain as she passed under the trees and hurtled up the flat path leading to

Taggart's cabin, but when she reached the door, at last she found her voice.

"Taggart!" Fear shrilled in her scream as she hammered with her fists on the door. "Let me in, let me in——"

He had obviously gone to bed; there wasn't a glimmer of light from any of his windows. Dear God, she thought, fighting back her sobs, what if he isn't here, what if he's at Zoe's, what if the bear is right now lumbering after me——?

A twig cracked behind her, and she whirled with a terrified gasp, but the moonlight washed white over the grassy clearing, and she could see nothing move. The sound must have been made by some scurrying little night creature...

Desperately, she turned toward the cabin again...to see a light playing and dancing out into the night from the kitchen window, to hear the quick heavy tread of a man's bare feet on the kitchen floor.

The door opened abruptly and Capri blinked as her face became the target of a torch's strong beam. She tried to speak, but all that came out was a ragged choking sound. Gasping for breath, she pressed her hands against her furiously pounding heart.

"You! What in tarnation's wrong, Jones? You sounded as if all the devils of hell were after you." Taggart swung the torch away from her, directing it along the empty path, and she saw him frown. He then flicked the powerful ray briefly over her body, and she saw his frown deepen as his gaze encompassed her clinging ivory silk nightshirt.

"I'm sorry," she managed at last, her voice a hoarse whisper. "It was a bear——"

"A *bear*?" Taggart sounded incredulous. Then she heard him swear under his breath. "For the love of heaven..."

He swept her into his kitchen as if she were a child, and, kicking the door shut, pulled out a chair and sat her down. Then after flicking off the torch, in the moonlight slanting in through the window he lit his lantern and set it in the centre of the table.

The only sound in the kitchen was a faint buzz from the lamp, and Capri's unsteady breathing. "I ... I didn't know ..." She curled her toes convulsively around the wooden slat supporting the front legs of her chair. "I didn't know there were ... bears on the island."

"There are a few in the woods, but we don't see them very often. They rarely venture down to this cleared area. Tell me what happened." He stood in front of her, hands on his hips. His hair was disheveled, his eyes still slightly bleary from sleep, but there was no mistaking the concern in his expression.

Capri noted that he was wearing a pair of jeans which he must have pulled on hastily when he jumped out of bed; they were zippered and buttoned, but the leather, silver-buckled belt he usually wore hung loose. He hadn't bothered to throw on a shirt—his chest was bare, the crisp gold curls glinting in the light from the lamp.

Capri hadn't realized she was shivering, but when she clasped her arms around herself she found her body was shaking uncontrollably. "I couldn't sleep," she managed. Then not wanting him to think her restlessness had been in any way due to him, added in a defensive tone, "I was hungry. I got up to make a snack and after I'd eaten I paid a visit to the outhouse. When I came back ..." She closed her eyes, but even with them shut she could still see the huge, towering figure of the bear—still see the menace in the black gaze, smell the foul odor. "When I came back he was standing right outside my door," she said shakily, "and when I saw him——"

"What did you have for your snack?"

Capri stared at him. What did *that* have to do with anything? "I ... I made a bacon sandwich, but ..."

For the first time, she saw a softening of the grim line that compressed Taggart's lips. "Bears do love bacon. It must have been lured down by the fragrance——"

"I'm not going back." Capri stared at him tensely, defiantly. "Not tonight. Not for anything."

"He'll be long gone by now, Jones," he returned reassuringly. "I'll take you to your cabin, and make sure you're safe. You've got nothing to worry a——"

"I'm not going back." Capri swallowed. She could hear the rising hysteria in her voice, but she could do nothing to control it. "Weren't you listening? I'm not moving from this cabin till daylight." She felt her teeth begin to chatter. She tried to clamp them together, but it didn't work. She still sounded—and felt!—as if she'd been swimming in Arctic waters!

Taggart looked at her for a long moment, and then, without a word, he moved over to the cupboard above the stove and took out a half full bottle of Chivas Regal and a glass. Capri watched fixedly as the Scotch gurgled into the glass, but she shook her head when he thrust it out to her.

"Uh-uh."

"Take it," he said curtly.

"I don't like Scotch."

"I don't give a damn whether you like it or not! Get it down you—in one gulp. You're in a state of shock."

Was that what was wrong with her? He was probably right. In any case, she didn't feel up to arguing. And the alcohol couldn't possibly make her feel any worse than she felt now.

She tossed back the fiery liquid, almost choking as it branded her throat. She shuddered. "I don't know how anyone can enjoy that stuff—I'd as soon swallow the Olympic flame!"

The faintest of smiles flickered across his lips. "I guess," he said wryly, "it's an acquired taste."

"I guess it is."

"You know," he murmured, with a taunting glint in his eye, "if you'd eaten the steak I barbecued for you, you wouldn't have been hungry, and you wouldn't have cooked bacon, and——"

"And this would never have happened." Capri played guiltily with the hem of her nightshirt. "I'm sorry," she said. "I feel badly about not finishing my meal. After you went to so much trouble to put on such a nice party. How did it go?"

"Oh, it went well," he said gravely.

"Did... anybody ask what had happened? I mean... why I didn't come back...?"

"Just Ellen."

Capri felt her lips twitch. "Ellen likes to know what's going on with everybody, doesn't she?" She hesitated, the smile fading. "What did you tell her?"

Taggart shrugged. "The truth."

"The truth?"

"I told her I wanted you to come back, but you hit me."

"You told her I hit you?"

Though Capri thought she had perfect control of her words, they came out in a slurred drawl. And all at once, she realized that reaction had set in... not only to her encounter with the bear, but to the whisky. Her limbs felt drained, her head light and fuzzy. She felt as if she was floating on a cloud.

"You did, didn't you?" His voice seemed to be coming from far away.

"Yes, but..." She tried to gather her thoughts. "I had a reason for hitting you... didn't I?"

"Don't *you* know?"

Capri nibbled on her lower lip. "Well, you did kiss me——"

"Ah. But it wasn't much of a kiss, was it?" There was a definite twinkle in his eye. "Didn't you say that on a scale of one to ten I would hover around a five?"

Capri tilted back her head. The whisky was having a very curious effect. It was making her feel sultry, seductive... She raised a hand and raked it through her long, tumbled hair as she recalled the blissful way his mouth had captured hers. "I did say you were a five, didn't I?" She felt her whole body relax, felt a slow, languorous heat spill through her veins. "I lied, Mr. Smith."

"You did?" His tone held the hint of a chuckle.

"Mm." Capri's mouth curved in a gentle, reminiscing smile. "You're *definitely* a ten..."

"Are you all right?"

Taggart's question came at her from the other end of a very long tunnel. "Yes," she mumbled. "I'm all right now." Her eyelids began to droop, and, despite her best efforts, she found herself letting them close. It was so much easier than trying to keep them open; they felt like lead. "Rude of me," she heard herself say, "to fall asleep in someone's kitchen."

She felt herself slipping sideways, but didn't have the strength to stop herself from falling. She heard Taggart swear, then felt him catching her in his strong arms, felt herself being lifted off the chair.

He was talking again, soothingly, as he walked with her. Her head lay against his chest, and she smiled as the covering of gold curls brushed her cheek. Then she was sinking down into a bed... between rumpled sheets that still held the scent and the warmth of Taggart's body. She didn't resist as he took her hands and placed them under the blankets.

She felt something caress her brow. His lips? A kiss? It made her feel safe, and cared for, the way she'd felt as a child, when her mother had tucked her in at night.

The next thing she heard was the sound of the bedroom door shutting.

Then there was nothing but darkness.

CHAPTER FIVE

"MISS JONES, I've brought you a cup of coffee..."

Capri yawned, and pulled the covers over her head as a woman's brisk voice cut into her dreams. "Thanks, Mary-Lou," she mumbled. "I'll wear my sapphire silk suit today. Did you remember to pick it up from the cleaners?"

"I'm afraid I didn't." The answering voice was tinged with sarcasm. "But I did fetch your robe from your cabin so you could get back there without being arrested for indecent exposure!"

What the...? Capri flung back the blankets and pushing her sleep-tousled hair back from her face, propped herself up on one elbow.

"Oh..." She was instantly wide awake as she looked up and saw, not Mary-Lou, her father's skinny, dark-haired housekeeper, but Zoe. The attractive blonde was holding out a steaming mug, and the scornful curl of her upper lip revealed even more clearly than her tone that serving coffee to another woman in her employer's bed was *not* part of her job description.

Capri forced a smile and gestured toward the bedside table. "Thanks." Her head buzzed with questions. Where was Taggart? Why hadn't *he* brought her the coffee? And, she wondered, with a bitchiness that astonished her, how could any woman look so damned sexy in a pair of men's navy overalls?

She let her glance slide away from Zoe's shrewd gaze, and noticed her white silk housecoat draped carelessly over the end of the bed. "And thanks for bringing my robe."

The blonde shrugged. "Taggart asked me to do it." It was quite obvious that chore, too, was one she hadn't relished.

"Where is he?"

Capri couldn't remember too much of what had happened after she'd drunk the Scotch... but she did have a dreamy recollection of being tucked in and kissed good night. It was amazing...she barely knew Taggart Smith, yet she'd trusted him implicitly—had gone to sleep in his bed like a baby. Her heart gave an apprehensive little kick as she anticipated seeing him again. Their relationship had taken a different turn last night; would she be able to get it back on a safe track?

She firmly blocked out the little voice in her head...an insidious little voice...that whispered, "Do you *want* to get it back on a safe track?"

"He's gone for the day. Fishing. With Sam." There was no mistaking the smug look on Zoe's face.

Capri was dismayed by the disappointment that coursed through her. "But..."

"But what?"

Capri reached for her mug, and sipped the coffee to give herself time to compose herself. "I didn't hear him get up this morning."

Zoe tossed her head and her braid swung around her perfect features. "Well, you wouldn't, would you?" Her lips curved in a secretive smile. "He didn't sleep here."

Capri's fingers tightened around the mug. She hadn't heard a thing after Taggart had closed her bedroom door, but she'd assumed he'd slept on the camp-bed in the living room. If he hadn't, then where...?

The triumphant gleam in Zoe's eyes seemed to hold the answer to her unspoken question. Capri had a sudden vivid image of Taggart and the blonde in bed, and with it came a sharp, ripping pain somewhere behind her breastbone. She leaned back weakly against her pillows.

She had never in her life experienced such a reaction . . .
What on earth was the *matter* with her?

She watched numbly as Zoe sauntered over to the
dresser, her buttocks round and taut under the navy
overalls. With her back to Capri, she began folding a
pile of her employer's underwear and shirts, and as she
put them away in a drawer she said, "I should warn you,
for your own good . . . don't get involved with Taggart."
She slid the drawer shut sharply before swinging around
again. Her eyes had darkened to the same deep walnut
color as her long, mascara'd eyelashes. "He's not
interested in long-term relationships."

Capri had been aware of the hostility emanating from
the other woman; now she felt the tension in the air
tighten even further. "I think you're being more than a
little presumptuous," she returned with an outraged
glare. "I'm a guest here on this island, and you are an
employee. It is absolutely none of your business
what——"

"They come over here every summer!" Zoe's glossy
pink lips twisted maliciously. "Uptight, sex-starved
females like yourself. And when they see Taggart they
just can't leave him alone. He's far too polite to tell them
to get lost—so I do it for him——"

Capri slammed the coffee mug onto the bedside table
with such force that some spilled over. "Get out," she
snapped.

Zoe lifted her perfect shoulders in an insolent shrug.
"Okay," she drawled. "But don't blame me if you get
hurt. I saw the two of you kissing on the jetty last night.
I just thought you ought to know . . . Taggart will never
let himself get serious about another woman . . . especially
a woman like you!" She paused, melodramatically.

Hating herself, Capri rose to the bait. "What do you
mean . . . a woman like me?" she asked icily.

"You are *exactly* the same type as his ex-wife!" Zoe
said triumphantly. "Oh, maybe you don't look like her—

she had blue-black hair and violet eyes—a dead ringer for the young Elizabeth Taylor—and a figure to match, but——"

"His ex-wife?" The astonished words were out before Capri could stop them. "I...I didn't know he'd been married," she added stiffly.

"Oh, yes, he was married all right," Zoe sneered, "to a rich society snob. I was only a teenager then, but Taggart's family and mine have always been friends, and I watched the whole thing happen. She thought she was being very clever—she didn't start trying to change him till *after* the wedding." Zoe laughed contemptuously. "She might as well have tried to turn the tide—it would have been easier." She shook her head and walked through the doorway into the kitchen, tossing over her shoulder as she went, "They were divorced within two years. Taggart Smith is his own man and *that* will never change."

As the outer door slammed behind her, Capri heard her own breath hiss out with the sound of a deflating balloon. She wished Zoe hadn't told her about Taggart. It was easier to think of him as a swinging bachelor than a divorcé. Easier to think of him as a man who sailed through life taking his pleasures where he might, rather than think of him as a man who had probably been badly hurt. No matter whose fault it was, a divorce always left scars.

In what way had his wife tried to change him? Capri frowned as she tried to remember what it was he had said when she'd suggested at the barbecue that he change his life-style... Something about first having to find a woman who would make that kind of sacrifice worthwhile.

She slid out of bed and reached for her robe. As she slipped her arms into the sleeves, and tied the belt, it suddenly dawned on her how very little she knew about Taggart Smith. When she had thought he was the care-

taker, she had wondered why he would settle for a job
so lacking in challenge. Now that she knew he owned
the island...an island that must be worth a fortune...she
couldn't help wondering how he had earned the money
to buy it.

And she couldn't help wondering what it was about
his life-style that he hadn't been prepared to sacrifice for
his wife.

And where did Zoe fit into the picture?

It disturbed Capri to realize how badly she wanted to
know the answers to her questions.

She worked till three, then changed into a buttercup-
yellow bikini and walked down to the beach. After carefully applying sunscreen, she spread out her towel, and
lay facedown on it, one cheek resting on her folded arms.
She would listen for Taggart's launch, she decided, and
at the first sound of its approach she would gather up
her things and hurry back to her cabin.

The sun was hot; it was sheer bliss to lie with her eyes
closed, listening to the rhythmic lapping of the waves.
But she would have to be careful she didn't fall asleep...

She started when she felt something tickling her back.

Squinting up against the bright sky, she felt her heart
skip a couple of beats as she saw Taggart looking down
at her. Wearing only a pair of khaki shorts, with his
figure outlined against the sun, he looked so incredibly
tall, so lean and rugged, that she felt her insides turn to
mush. Damn, she thought irritably, she must have dozed
off after all...

With a defeated sigh, she watched as he picked up the
fat tube of Lancôme sunscreen lying at the edge of her
towel.

"You came prepared," he murmured. "I can see
you're a woman who doesn't take risks."

Capri sensed the underlying implication in his words.
She decided it was best to ignore it. "It's common

knowledge that the rays of the sun are very dangerous.'' She turned away from him and laid her other cheek against her folded arms. "I don't want to get burned.''

Her pulse quickened as he stepped across her body and got down on his haunches beside her. "Even if you use sunscreen,'' he murmured, trailing a finger down her spine, "you can never be one hundred percent safe.''

"I know there's still a risk..." she wriggled in a vain effort to get away from his disturbing touch "...but it's one I'm willing to take. I love the sun.''

"Ah—love!'' His voice had taken on a mocking timbre. "What people will risk in the name of love.''

Capri sneaked a look at him from under her lashes, and saw that his expression was cynical.

"You don't believe in love?''

He unscrewed the lid of the tube and squeezed an inch of gel into his palm. "Oh, yes, I do believe in love, Jones——''

"You do?''

"Why the astonishment?'' He replaced the lid and tossed the tube on to the towel.

Capri had swept her hair up into a top-knot before coming to the beach; now she felt her skin tingle as Taggart began smoothing the gel over her nape. "It's just that Zoe said...''. She closed her eyes. His touch was firm yet gentle...and decidedly erotic... She tensed all her muscles in a supreme effort to keep from squirming with pleasure as his fingers slid down and began working sensually over her shoulder blades...

"Zoe said what?''

"Zoe said...you had once been married, but the marriage didn't work out.'' She stiffened further as he untied the strap of her bikini top and began, with lazy circling movements, to oil her back. "I just thought——''

"You just thought that since I'd been burned I'd keep clear of that particular fire.''

"Something like that."

"You're right, I was burned." He retied the bikini top and Capri breathed a sigh of relief. "And I *am* keeping clear of the fire. *Well* clear. But I'm not denying the *existence* of the fire, Jones." He began gliding his palms around the curve of her body, just above her waist, in a gentle massaging movement. "It still draws me, tempts me. And maybe if I get cold enough I'll be crazy enough to forget how it damn well hurts, and walk blindly into it again."

"You're comparing falling in love to walking into a *fire*?"

"In a sense." His fingertips were dangerously close to the outer swell of her breasts. "But now it's my turn to ask questions. You said you weren't interested in getting married. Have you gone through a messy divorce too?"

Capri shook her head, afraid to speak, in case the wrong sound came out...though his fingers were several inches from her nipples, she could feel the sensitive tips pearl as if he had already caressed them.

"No? But you've been hurt...by somebody."

Under his touch, her skin felt as if it were on fire. And the fire was spreading inward, along every nerve in her body, to a spot deep inside her...like a flame hissing relentlessly toward a keg of dynamite.

Alarm bells jangled loudly in her head; she would, she knew, be a fool to ignore them!

In one swift, fluid movement, she pushed his hands away, and, rolling over, sat up. She bent her legs and looped her arms round them.

"That'll do," she said, her lips tightening into a prim line.

"What about the front?" His tone was boyishly hopeful.

"I can manage that myself."

He sighed, regretfully.

Capri stared out at the ocean. She felt as dizzy as if a giant had just taken her by the scruff of the neck and shaken her... hard.

"Who was he?" Taggart sat down beside her with his legs apart, his elbows resting on his bent knees. From the corner of her eye, Capri could see his well-shaped hands dangling casually over his Reeboks.

"Who was...who?" Purposely she adopted a slightly vague tone.

"Whoever it was who has made you afraid of...fire."

A sea gull wheeled overhead with a sudden raucous cry. "I really don't want to talk about it..."

"He must have meant a great deal to you." Taggart's tone was quiet...and gently coaxing.

Capri felt a smarting behind her eyelids. She had never been able to talk about Jamie since his death... not even with her father. Why would she talk about him to someone who was almost a stranger?

"He was my other half..."

For a moment, she could hardly believe the husky whisper had come from her own lips. But, of course, it had. What was it about this man that had made her confide even that much to him? And—even more bewildering—why was she almost overwhelmed by a sudden relentless urge to tell him more? To tell him that her other half was not a lover, as he probably imagined, but her twin brother Jamie, whom she'd loved more than life itself? She wanted to tell him that when Jamie had died at twenty-one, she had wanted to die too. Only the thought of leaving her father alone had kept her from——

"I'm sorry." He swore quietly. "I've made you cry..."

Roughly she brushed the back of her hand across her eyes, shaking her head in denial as she did so.

"It seems," he said in a deliberately casual tone, "as if you and I are both eligible to join the CWW."

"The...what's that?" Capri knew he was trying to lighten the moment, and she was grateful for it.

"The Club for the Walking Wounded. Haven't you heard of it?"

"No..."

"Oh, let me explain, then! The only qualification necessary for membership is that a person must have suffered a lethal blow to the heart."

"That's all?" Despite her best attempts to match his teasing tone, Capri couldn't prevent a note of bitterness from creeping into her voice. "And does that entitle one to life membership?"

"Now there's a depressing thought. Would you expect it to? Would you want it to?"

Capri had never allowed herself to look very far into the future...her future. Now she did...and saw a picture of herself thirty years down the road, old, lonely, not loving...not loved. She shivered. "It sounds like a death sentence," she said, almost to herself.

"Doesn't it, though!"

She forced her mind to shut out the dismal picture. In an attempt to divert the focus of conversation away from herself, she asked, "How long is it since your divorce?"

"Six years."

Capri spoke her thoughts aloud, barely aware that she was doing so. "Zoe said your wife was...very beautiful."

"Susan?" He scooped up a handful of sand, and let it trickle out slowly from between his long, hard fingers. "Yes," he said in a tone that gave nothing away, "yes, she was beautiful."

How could she feel jealous of a woman she'd never seen? Capri didn't know the answer to her unspoken question...she only knew that she'd felt a sharp ache in her heart as she listened to his casual words. She decided it was time to change the subject completely.

"Zoe also said you told her to bring me coffee and my robe. Thank you."

"My pleasure. I checked the area around your cabin after you fell asleep——"

"You didn't see the bear?" Capri asked anxiously.

"No. I guess he was even more scared than you were!"

"I'll never cook bacon at night again," she said fervently.

He chuckled. "No, I don't imagine you will. Did you sleep well?"

"Mm." Capri leaned over to straighten the towel, hoping to hide the rise of color to her cheeks. "Yes, thanks..." She paused. *Ask him.* "After you checked that the bear had gone, why didn't you come back to the cabin?" Did you go to Zoe's? The question trembled, unspoken.

"Because you were in my bed."

"But——"

"You didn't want to share it, did you?"

Capri knew her cheeks must be as red as a peony rose. "Of course not. It's just... well, you could have used the camp-bed in the living room."

"I decided it wasn't safe."

"Not safe from...oh." She bridled. "You needn't have worried about *me*... I wouldn't have compromised you——"

"Silly girl, I wasn't worried that *I* wouldn't be safe...I was worried that *you* wouldn't be. After seeing you in that alluring silk nightshirt, I knew I'd better give you a wide berth. That's why I didn't bring the coffee and robe myself. That's why I spent the day fishing."

Their gazes met, and clung. Capri almost gasped aloud as she felt the power of the sexual currents sizzling between them. It took all the self-control she possessed not to let her body sway toward him; she felt as if he'd lassooed her with an invisible rope of fine silk and was pulling her, drawing her to him.

Hypnotized, she watched as he leaned forward. Time seemed frozen, and she was aware of nothing but the two of them. And in the instant before his lips touched hers, she could see tiny white flecks in his blue irises, could see every individual lash fringing his wonderful eyes, could see a smokiness in his gaze that sent a splinter of answering desire slicing through her. And then his lips brushed hers in a kiss so light that it was like the caress of a baby's fingertip. "I hoped," he whispered softly, "that if I kept away from you I'd be able to get you out of my mind."

Capri couldn't have moved if her life had depended on it. The moment he'd touched her she was under his spell. A slow heat began spreading through her veins as he traced her upper lip with the tip of his tongue, and then began teasing his way along her jawline. "And did it work?" Her voice was breathless.

"No, damn you," he answered huskily, "it didn't."

She closed her eyes. His breath was hot against her skin, his breathing shallower than it had been a moment ago. How neatly he had avoided telling her where he had slept. But perhaps there was nothing to hide. Perhaps he hadn't gone to Zoe... Capri was astonished at how desperately she wanted to believe that.

When his lips returned to hers, claiming them in a kiss that was sweet, persuasive, irresistible, she felt herself turning sideways into his embrace. It was the summer's day, she told herself weakly, that was making her feel so deliciously languorous, so erotically receptive... the lulling sound of the ocean, the heady scents from the wildflowers and the ocean, the sun on her near-naked flesh.

Somewhere up above, she heard the drone of a small plane. She stirred, knowing she should pull away, but she didn't have the strength.

Taggart did.

He cupped his hands around her shoulders and then after a moment slid them down her arms, and clasped her fingers. Drawing them to his lips, he pressed a kiss on each palm, sending shafts of pleasure through her. "You know what I think?" His eyes were bluer than the sky above him.

"No," she whispered. "What?" They were so close that she found herself inhaling his breath: the knowledge made her giddy.

"I think that the time is wrong, and the place is wrong, for something that's so...right." Squeezing her hands gently, he released them, and, running his lips over her brow in a fleeting caress, got to his feet. He didn't say anything for a moment, just looked down at her with a slow, intimate smile that made her heart do a couple of back flips, and then he murmured, "What are you doing tonight?"

"Tonight?" Capri tried to shake off her feeling of lethargy. "I was planning to work. I have a report I'd like to finish——"

"Take the evening off." He rested his hands lightly on his hips. "I didn't have any luck when we were fishing today, but Sam caught a beauty. Ellen's going to broil it and they want us to join them for dinner—I volunteered to pass on the invitation."

"Oh...do please thank them for me, but I'm falling behind in the schedule I set myself. I really have to get caught up——"

"You have to stop to eat, don't you?"

"Well, yes, but..."

He grinned, as easily as if the intimate interlude between them had never happened. "May as well eat with us, Jones. You can work afterward. Oh, and by the way, wear that blue sweater you had on last night, the one with your initials on the pocket..."

"The blue sweater? Why?" With the question, she knew she'd accepted the invitation. What had happened to her common sense?

"You'll find out... later. I'll come to your cabin and we can walk over together. About six?"

"Fine." As soon as she'd spoken, Capri wanted to snatch the word back... but she didn't. She shook her head helplessly as he moved away. In her own environment in Houston, in the office or at home, she was assertive, positive, self-disciplined. Why was it that here on this island... and more particularly when she was around this man... she became spineless and dithery? Had she lost the ability to say "No"?

She began gathering up her things... but found her gaze following Taggart as he strolled away toward his cabin. She whispered a frustrated exclamation. The more she saw of him, the more she liked him. He was warm and witty, strong yet tender, and...

And he was drawing feelings from her that she wanted to keep suppressed.

She was teetering on the edge of a dangerous fire. A fire she had sworn to herself that she would scrupulously avoid.

Tonight she would have to be careful that she didn't let it draw her too close. The last thing she wanted to do was to fall in!

"I've never tasted fish so deliciously fresh before!" Alone in the kitchen with Ellen, Capri dried the last of the plates that had been used at dinner. "You're a *wonderful* cook."

"Why, thanks, Capri." Ellen let the soapy water out of the sink and dried her hands on a small towel. "Taggart's a great chef too, isn't he? Wasn't that steak last night out of this world...?" Her words trailed away and she uttered a vexed exclamation. "Oh... I'm *sorry*. I didn't mean to talk about last night."

"That's all right." Capri put a reassuring hand on Ellen's forearm. "You must have wondered what was going on when I left before I'd even eaten! It was just that when I found out Taggart had let me go on believing he was the caretaker, I was furious with him. Later, when I cooled down a bit, I realized I had behaved childishly by blowing up at him...he was only having a bit of fun. And to be truthful I guess I asked for it, behaving like some temperamental prima donna when I found him lying in bed the afternoon I arrived!"

"He followed you last night after you fled." Ellen's green eyes were bright.

Capri grimaced. "Yes."

"Then Zoe went to look for him—she said it was because she couldn't find the second case of beer but I saw it later and it was right there in the kitchen—and when she came back she looked like thunder." Ellen didn't say, What happened? but the question was in her eyes, and Capri couldn't bring herself to ignore it.

"Zoe saw us...Taggart and myself...on the jetty. He was—er—we were..."

"*Kissing?*" Ellen's face lit up eagerly.

Capri hesitated, then thought, What the heck! "Yes," she muttered. "Kissing."

"Oh, that's wonderful——"

"What's so wonderful?" Taggart's teasing voice behind them made them both swivel around.

Why did he have to be so damned sexy-looking? Capri thought irritably. His blond hair, tanned skin, and laughing blue eyes were a combination that was totally irresistible—did he also have to have a smile that set her heart spinning, and a body that stirred to rebellious life every one of her baser animal instincts?

"The fish," she said, with an airy gesture. "I was just saying to Ellen I'd never tasted such fresh fish before. She agreed it was wonderful."

His grin widened, and Capri realized he knew she was lying. But he didn't pursue the matter. "It *was* good," he said, and glanced at his watch as he spoke.

Capri noticed him frown. It was just after nine... was he planning to leave? She was horrified at the thrill of anticipation that raced through her. All evening—despite her best efforts—she'd been remembering what he'd said at the beach, about that not being the time nor the place for their kiss, and it had been impossible not to wonder when and where... and if!... he intended to resume his seductive advances. Her inner tension had been building relentlessly; now it reached a crescendo as she anticipated his walking her back to her cabin. Would she be strong enough to resist his advances—if he made any?

"It's time you were in bed, Ellen," he was saying. "Sam told me you weren't feeling too well earlier."

Capri momentarily forgot her own anxieties as with a stab of self-reproach she noticed the lines of strain around the other woman's mouth, and the dark circles under her eyes. "Oh, Ellen, why didn't you say something?"

"I'm all right." Ellen smiled dismissively. "If I'm tired, it's because this baby's a lot bigger than Miranda was at eight months..."

"Whatever the reason," Taggart put his arm around her bulky body and gave her a hug, "I'm giving you strict orders to go straight to bed. Jones and I have to leave now anyway—we're going to take a walk along the beach..."

As he cocked a self-assured eyebrow in Capri's direction, she felt her heartbeats flutter erratically, but before she could protest Ellen spoke.

"What a lovely idea! It'll be beautiful by the water. We've been so lucky with the weather... Sammy," she called, "come on through. Our guests are leaving."

As her husband came into the kitchen, Ellen opened the fridge door and took out the bottle of white wine that had been on the table at dinnertime. "Here, Taggart, take this with you—it'll just sit there if you don't. Sam prefers beer and I don't drink while I'm pregnant. And here's a couple of plastic cups...you and Capri can have a picnic on the beach..."

Capri felt as if she were being swept along by forces beyond her control. A picnic on the beach... the heady effect of wine, coupled with the even headier effect of his closeness...? She felt a swell of panic rising inside her at the prospect. What was she going to do?

As they left the cabin, Capri felt the sweet-scented breeze caress her face and instead of putting on her navy jacket she draped it over her shoulders. "I thought it would have cooled off by now," she said lightly.

"It's a perfect night," Taggart replied, looking down at her with a lazy smile as he slid the cups over the neck of the bottle. "Much warmer than is usual for the time of year." He stuffed his free hand into the pocket of his jeans, and Capri could hear him whistling under his breath.

How strange that his relaxed attitude—the thing about him that had so irritated her at first—was now the very thing that seemed to draw her to him! Was it because she herself was so intense? She knew, of course, that opposites were said to attract...and there was no denying her attraction to him! And where was that going to lead her? If she'd been unable to resist his kisses in broad daylight, how could she possibly expect to resist them in the moonlight? To go and sit with him on the beach was asking for trouble.

A few moments ago, she'd been asking herself what she was going to do. How ridiculous...there was only one thing she *could* do.

She waited till they were abreast of her cabin, and then she halted. "The Walterses are a nice couple, aren't they? I had a wonderful evening.'' She put one hand over her mouth as she feigned a yawn. ''I was planning to do some work after I came home, but I think I'll have an early night——''

''Hey, not so fast.'' As she turned away from him, Taggart reached out for her hand and pulled her back. ''Where do you think you're going?''

Capri tried to sound casual. ''Oh, I thought that since you had such a disturbed night last night you'd want to turn in early too——''

He held up the bottle. ''And have you tell Ellen tomorrow that I didn't share the wine with you? No way, Jones.'' His eyes teased her. ''I'm not going to fall into that little trap!''

He tightened his grip, and Capri could feel a prickly tingling running up her arm from his fingers. The sensation spread through her whole body, exciting and yet terrifying her, as if she was about to dive into a beautiful blue pool, not knowing exactly how deep it was. Every sane and sensible instinct warned her to pull away from him while she could. She knew that if she did he wouldn't struggle with her. She already knew him well enough to be certain he would never force her to walk with him— or do anything else with him—against her will. All she had to do was let him know that she was serious about wanting to return to her cabin, and he would release her.

For the space of a long, breathless second, she hesitated . . . and then—whether bewitched by the moonlight and the musky closeness of his body or driven by the mindless urgings of her own hormones, she wasn't sure— at any rate, she ignored the prudent, sober parts of her brain which were screaming at her not to be a fool, and she fell in with his step.

He reached over and kissed the top of her head, and she guessed he was letting her know that he had sensed her uncertainty . . . and that he was glad she'd decided to accompany him. At his gentle touch, she felt her apprehension alleviated by a shiver of trembling elation.

The terrain was shadowy and uneven, and without his support she knew she would have stumbled. His grip was firm, protective, guiding—she had never been with a man who made her feel so safe.

Nor, she acknowledged, with a tightening of her nerves, had she ever been with one who was quite so dangerous.

Dangerous to her peace of mind. And a threat to the shield she'd erected around her heart.

CHAPTER SIX

AS THEY reached the flat sandy beach and she no longer had to concentrate on where she was stepping, Capri found herself thinking of her father and his plans for her—plans that up till now she had managed to thwart. How ironic it was that the very first time she had gone her own way and chosen her own vacation spot she had ended up in the very kind of situation she had been so determined to avoid——

"A penny for them."

"Oh." Capri shrugged, hesitated for a moment, and then said, "I was thinking about my father."

"Are your parents both alive?"

"No, my mother died when I was fourteen."

He made a sympathetic sound. "I should think that must be one of the worst ages for a girl to lose her mother. She's on the brink of becoming a woman herself—a confusing time...and a time when she must often need someone close she can talk to."

"You're right," she murmured. "The timing couldn't have been worse."

"Had she been ill before she died?"

"No, she was never sick...she never had time to be sick!" Capri bit her lip. Was she really talking about her mother? She always avoided talking about her, or Jamie—even with her father, though many times she'd suspected it might have helped alleviate his grief. Her own sorrow had been too deep. Too deep...and too selfish? She'd never thought of it in that way before. Ashamed, she pushed aside the niggling feelings of guilt as Taggart spoke.

"She worked?" he asked.

"She didn't have a regular job, if that's what you mean. Madeline Jones, clocking in from nine to five?" Capri shook her head and chuckled wryly. "Might as well have asked an eagle to lock itself in a cage. And she was like an eagle...strong, and wild, and free. But she didn't go through life taking and not giving! She more than paid her dues to society by her fund-raising activities—I used to think she was on the board of every hospital in Houston! A Maddy Jones smile could raise enough money to build a whole new wing!"

"And what did this charming...eagle...do when she wasn't fund-raising?"

Capri smiled at the slightly mocking tone in his voice. "Can't you guess? She was flying! She had a small plane of her own, and my first memory is of watching it spiraling down from the sky. I knew she was in it, and I thought it was going to crash. I was only four and of course I didn't realize she was in complete control, so the sight terrified me. I was hysterical. Emily—my nanny—managed to calm me down before my mother finally landed, but I sensed—even at that tender age— that it would disappoint her if she knew how I felt, so I hid it."

"And kept hiding it?"

"Right. She never guessed how I hated her flying. From that very first time, I was afraid she was going to kill herself." Capri felt her throat muscles tighten. "Eventually she did. She was flying her plane in a race and something went wrong..."

"Were you there?"

"I was in school. My father came for me." Capri clamped her teeth together as she remembered the haggard expression on Jake's face. Jamie had been at the same school, and, together, they'd gone to look for him. It was the lunch hour, and though they looked in the cafeteria he wasn't with his friends. They eventually

found him in the students' parking lot, alone, running
a reverent hand over a magnificent Harley Davidson
motor-bike belonging to one of the older boys. He had
broken down when he'd heard the news, and the three
of them had stood there, arms around each other, three
hearts breaking...

"Watch out...don't trip..." As Taggart's warning
words broke into her aching thoughts, he released her
hand and, putting his arm around her, pulled her against
him and half lifted her over a pile of tangled seaweed.
Then, instead of taking her hand again, he kept his arm
around her shoulders.

Capri blinked back the tears that were welling in her
eyes. Determinedly pushing her memories aside, and
swallowing the painful lump in her throat, she said,
"Enough about me. How about you? Are *your* parents
still alive? Oh, I forgot," she managed a teasing little
laugh, "they kicked you out when you were eleven.
You've probably no idea where they are."

In the brief pause before he responded, Capri sensed
that he would have liked to hear more about her family.
But he obviously decided to respect her not-so-subtle attempt to side-track him, for, after a moment, he grinned
and said, "As a matter of fact, I don't. When Dad re-
tired last year, they bought a motor home, and they've
been on the road ever since. They're somewhere in
California at the moment—or it could be Oregon!"

"Half a sec..." Capri ducked out from under his arm,
and, sliding off her sandals, dangled them from her
hand. "Sand in them...uncomfortable..." She stepped
a little away from him as she resumed walking. "What
kind of work did your father do?" She hoped Taggart
would keep his distance, but before she knew it he had
closed the space between them and draped his arm
around her again.

"He was an accountant with a Calgary firm."

"Do you have any brothers or sisters?"

"Just an older sister—Tracy. She and her husband both teach English in a Calgary high school. They have a ten-year-old son. Trace has had a couple of historical romances published—her ambition is to write full-time, eventually, but she's not quite ready to take the plunge yet."

"Oh. So that's how you were able to advise me about my 'romance writing'! Sounds as if you have a nice family. And you..." she went on as nonchalantly as she could. "Now that I know you're not a caretaker, are you going to tell me what you *really* do?"

"My partner and I have our own company in Calgary. I like being my own boss—means I can come to the island whenever I need a break. And now that I know you're not a romance writer..." smoothly he switched the conversation away from himself "...are you going to tell me what *you* really do?"

Capri looked out to sea. Way in the distance, she could see lights twinkling...some small boat, or perhaps a lighthouse, she mused absently. His response had been cagey; she didn't want to trespass if he had a reason for his reluctance to talk about himself...and she herself wanted to keep her response equally vague. "I work for a big company in Houston. In administration."

That seemed to satisfy him. He didn't pursue the subject, but stopped walking, and she realized they'd reached the end of the beach. They were standing on a sheltered grassy spot, right above the sand, and as she looked around she couldn't help thinking it was like a corner of paradise. The ocean and sand were brushed with silver, and the full moon hung in the sky like a perfect ivory disc on a swathe of purple velvet.

"This is as far as we can go," Taggart murmured, his breath warm against her cheek. "Let me have your jacket."

She could barely hear the lapping of the waves along the shore for the erratic thudding of her heartbeats as he took the garment and draped it on the grass for her.

They had talked together that afternoon of their wariness of fire . . . the fire that was love. Now, as he sank down beside her jacket, and held up a hand to her with a soft, "Come here, Jones," a pulse flickered tremulously at her throat.

Love wasn't the only fire of which she was wary; there was another which was, in a different and unique way, equally perilous. And as she tossed her thongs on the grass and let him pull her down beside him she could see that fire smoldering in his eyes—the fire of desire.

The flame was tantalizing and seductive.

Would she be able to resist it?

She sat cross-legged, watching from under her lashes as he poured wine into the two plastic cups. Her breathing was regular . . . so why did she feel so breathless?

"Let's drink a toast," he murmured. "To the Walterses, for enticing you away from your computer tonight."

There was a glittering intensity in his eyes that set something quivering deep in her womb. Dizzily, she took the cup from him. His magnetism, his sexuality, were incredible—he hadn't even touched her, yet she felt herself sway helplessly toward him. She ached to run her fingertips over his perfectly molded lips, ached to caress the firm line of his jaw with her palm——

With a little shiver, she straightened. Raising her cup to her mouth, she made a pretense of drinking, but barely sipped the alcohol—she was already feeling tipsy enough without adding bubbles of intoxication to her veins! Thankful of the shadows created by the moon, she casually set her cup down into the grass by her side, and, with a surreptitious turn of her wrist, tilted out all the wine.

"So, tell me," she asked, her nervousness making her say the first thing that came into her head, "why did you want me to wear this blue sweater tonight?"

"I'm glad you asked." He had sprawled down on the grass, and was lying on one side, supporting himself on his elbow as he looked up at her. "The initials on the pocket intrigue me," he said.

"They do?" Capri glanced down at the silver CJ. "I can't think why."

"Seeing them brought back happy memories."

"Of what?"

"My kindergarten teacher."

"Did she wear a sweater like this?"

"Good Lord, no! The Sparrow never wore anything but polyester pant suits—and those were invariably mustard or magenta!"

"Then what...?"

"She taught us the alphabet by printing out the letters for each of us on blue bristol board—exactly the same ice blue as your sweater—in silver, with a fat felt marker. Before we were allowed to copy them into our workbook——" he finished his wine and laid the cup on the grass beside the bottle "—we had to trace over each letter, like this..."

He reached across the space between them and, before Capri could anticipate what he was going to do, with the tip of one long finger he outlined the monogram on her breast pocket. Through her sweater, she felt the pressure of his touch on the soft silk of her nipple...and through her body she felt a raking shudder of raw desire that made her gasp.

She twisted away from him, trying to hide her dismay. "You're not a little boy now." Her voice shook. "Don't you think it's time you stopped playing games?"

He stared at her for a long moment, his expression unreadable. Then he rolled over onto his back, and as he clasped his hands behind his head he closed his eyes. "Who's the one playing games?" he asked quietly.

"What do you mean?" The raking shudder had passed, but had left in its wake a swift throbbing in her breasts, a quivering tightness that in its own way was just as alarming. Capri hugged herself, pressing her arms against the traitorously jutting peaks in a futile effort to force them back to their former petal-soft innocence.

"A few minutes ago," Taggart said, "you were undecided as to whether to come with me or not. But you made your decision, and you came. In view of what happened between us on the beach this afternoon . . . tell me, if you didn't expect me to make a pass, what *did* you expect?"

"Certainly not a writing lesson——" she began in a deliberately flippant tone, but he broke in.

"There's a time for humor, Jones, and this is not it. I didn't ask what you *didn't* expect. I asked you what you *did* expect."

Capri swallowed. He wasn't going to allow her to waffle her way out of this. What was she going to say?

"I'm waiting." His eyes were still closed—and as she looked down at him Capri could see a nerve quiver just under one brow. So . . . he wasn't quite as relaxed as he'd have her believe! The knowledge gave her confidence.

"You're right," she said. "I . . . I wasn't sure whether I should come along the beach with you tonight. And my decision to come was . . . impulsive." She frowned. "I don't know the answer to your question. I didn't really have time to think it through in my own mind."

She watched warily as he opened his eyes. "That's better." He smiled. "There's nothing like a bit of honesty to clear the air. Now, just one more thing."

Capri breathed a sigh of relief. That hadn't been as bad as she'd expected. He was right. It was stupid to play games. "Yes?"

"Normally, when I decide to kiss a woman, I don't ask her permission first. I'm no Casanova but I do have enough experience to read signals—whether they be given with the eyes, the voice, or the body." He sat up. "You're different from any female I've met before. I can't read your signals. They're confused. And I have to assume they're confused because *you*'re confused——"

"What's the point in all——?"

He pressed a fingertip to her mouth, stopping her words and leaving the imprint of his skin on her lips. "I don't want to take something...anything...you're not ready to give, and, since I'm a great believer in the direct approach, I'm going to put my cards on the table." His eyes glinted in the moonlight, giving him a ruthless appearance. "You're the most unconsciously erotic woman I've ever met, and I've been wanting to make love to you from the very first moment I laid eyes on you——"

"Oh, *really*?" Though her tone was cold, Capri felt her cheeks begin to burn. In her twenty-five years she had often been called beautiful...but no one had ever called her erotic before! The knowledge that Taggart found her so set the blood churning wildly through her veins...a fact she certainly didn't want him to discover. "Well," she said stiffly, "you may want to make love to me, but you'll have to learn that in this life you can't have everything you want. I do have *some* say in the matter!"

"I agree."

"Well, aren't you generous!"

He ignored her sniping comment. "So you can relax...you needn't be afraid you'll have to dodge any more passes."

"Thank you, kind sir!" Capri snapped.

"Don't get me wrong," he said smoothly. "You and I *are* eventually going to make love. I'd stake my life on it. But before that happens I want to be sure you want it as much as I do. And the only way to accomplish that is to toss the ball into your court.

"To put it bluntly, Jones...I made my move and you checked it.

"The next move is yours."

* * *

Hell will freeze over first! Go look for your sexy blonde caretaker if you want a cheap thrill—she's obviously panting to go to bed with you...

Capri's furious response still rang in her ears as she tried to concentrate on her report next morning. Making a determined effort to block the ugly scene from her mind, she stared fixedly at the statistics on her computer screen.

She had finally finished inputting all the information. And the extremely detailed figures, which she'd had the personnel department gather for her during the past year, showed quite clearly that absenteeism among the female employees at Jones Oil was significantly more frequent than that among the men. They also showed that women with children under the age of six had the worst record, some having lost an incredible fifty to a hundred work days in the twelve-month period. And the reasons for these absences? Capri sighed and shook her head. Though many of them stemmed from children's illnesses, a greater percentage had resulted from problems with day care.

The former Jones Oil could obviously not do much about, but the day care problems...

Frowning, Capri tapped her fingers on the surface of the table. Productivity and efficiency suffered when workers took time off—and when they quit altogether, as many of the female workers had done at Jones Oil because of child care problems, training new staff was extremely costly. Hadn't Ellen said something about day care being provided at her place of work? How would Jake and the board—who were mostly men—react if she were to suggest on-site day care at Jones Oil? Surely the cost could be balanced favorably against the cost of retraining?

If her own experience of life had been different, she mused absently, she would probably have married and had children; she would not have wanted to give up her career, and being able to take her child to work with her would have been the ideal situation.

She suddenly had a vivid picture of herself, rushing up the steps of the Jones Oil building, a baby in her arms. A little boy, with fair hair, blue eyes, and a butter-melting smile, just like——

With a distraught exclamation, she got up from the table, and, opening the fridge door, she took out the jug of iced tea she'd made earlier. Half filling a glass and cradling it in her hands, she slumped back onto her chair.

It was no use. No matter where she tried to focus her thoughts, they always swung back...to Taggart Smith.

Why couldn't she stop thinking about him?

Last night it had been the same. She couldn't stop thinking about what had happened between them on the beach. She had hardly slept a wink, bitterly regretting saying what she had said about Zoe. Her accusation concerning the blond woman had been totally uncalled-for.

And as she'd tossed and turned, she had also ack-nowledged—reluctantly—that her anger had been a side-product of her crushing disappointment. Though she'd rejected Taggart when he'd made his move, she hadn't expected him to be so easily put off...and hadn't realized till that moment just how much she'd been anticipating his kisses. But they were not to be hers—unless she put *her* cards on the table and confessed that she wanted them!

A knock at the door interrupted her thoughts, and she felt her nerves tense. After Taggart's bold challenge, and her angry outburst, she had grabbed up her sandals and stormed back along the beach. He had been right behind her all the way, but he hadn't tried to catch up with her.

She had been very sure he wouldn't seek her out today, and she knew she should have been pleased. Didn't she want to leave this island as heart-free as when she'd arrived? So why had she been feeling as thwarted as a little girl who'd been allowed just one lick of a lollipop before it was taken away and put on a high shelf where she couldn't reach it?

Placing her glass on the table, she got up and stepped quickly toward the sink, where a small round mirror sat on the wide sill. She hadn't put on any makeup—the air was so stiflingly hot that perspiration had beaded on her skin as soon as she'd washed her face—but her cheeks had a rosy glow from her sunbathing session the day before, and her eyes were clear and sparkling. Deftly, she fluffed the sweat-damp hair from her nape, and glossed her lips with the tip of her tongue.

Another knock, this time louder, had her traitorous legs twitching to run eagerly to the door. Carefully smoothing a hand over her yellow T-shirt and matching shorts, she controlled her pace. "Coming," she called lightly as she walked across the kitchen, and, schooling her features into an artificially questioning expression, she opened the door.

"Hi, Capri." Ellen stood on the bottom step, waving a leafy branch in front of her face like a fan, and panting just a little. "Miranda's sleeping, and Sammy's babysitting. I know it's early but I just wanted to..." She hesitated, her breasts heaving under her green, tentlike dress. "I just wanted to ask how you and Taggart enjoyed your picnic last night," she finally said in a rush.

"Good morning, Ellen." Capri refused to acknowledge the sharp stab of disappointment that had pierced her when she saw her visitor wasn't Taggart. "I was just having some iced tea. Would you like to join me?"

"Would I ever! It's so close today that I can hardly breathe. The air's uncannily still." Ellen tossed her leafy fan on the top step and walking heavily across the room, lowered herself onto one of the chairs. "So——" she propped an elbow on the table and rested her chin in her cupped hand as she slanted Capri a quizzical glance

"—what happened last night? Did the two of you have a fight?"

"How on earth did you guess?" The words were out before Capri could stop them. She grimaced. "Am I so transparent?"

Ellen shook her head. "I have to confess I bumped into Taggart a little while ago and when I asked *him* how the picnic had gone, he seemed a bit . . . edgy. "Curiosity killed the cat!' was all he said. I thought he wasn't his usual self . . . you know how he is normally—teasing, lots of fun."

Capri set Ellen's iced tea in front of her and, topping up her own glass, sat down at the other end of the table. "You know him quite well, Ellen?"

"Sammy and I met him seven years ago, the first summer we came to Blueberry. Our holidays don't always coincide with his occasional trips here, but they have done often enough that we've come to enjoy each other's company." She shrugged. "We don't know *that* much about him, really. He's very neighborly, as you must have noticed, and for the most part frank and open . . . but when it comes to his life away from here, he's very private."

"Do you know what kind of business he's in?"

Ellen made a vague gesture with her glass. "I can only guess. I know he travels all over the world, and I know that when he comes to Blueberry Island he's always exhausted . . . sleeps for a couple of days sometimes! Jet lag, I suppose." She ran the fingers of one hand through her gingery curls. "He's a bit of a mystery man . . ."

"Mystery man?"

Ellen glanced quickly toward the open door, and lowered her voice as she said, "I went over to his cabin one afternoon, a couple of years ago, to give him some blueberry jelly I'd made, and he wasn't in but the door was open, so I thought I'd drop it on the kitchen table. As I was leaving, I heard a man's voice in the living

room, and, thinking it was Taggart, I knocked on the
door and went in. There was nobody there. I thought I
must have been imagining things, then I heard the voice
again. It seemed to be coming from inside a cupboard!
I investigated...and found a VHF radio! Someone was
trying to make contact—sounded pretty urgent. As I left,
I met Taggart coming along the path, so I told him what
I'd heard and he just said 'Thanks.'" Ellen lifted her
shoulders in a "who knows?" gesture. "'Thanks.'" That
was all. No explanation...but he lost no time getting
inside that cabin, I can tell you! I never would have
guessed he could move so fast...he's usually so relaxed
and easygoing. And he was gone within the hour."

"Gone?"

"Gone. To the mainland. We didn't see him again
that summer. But you know how nosy I am—the next
year, I tried to find out what was going on. Taggart—
in his own charming way—stonewalled all my
questions!"

"Intriguing..." Capri absently ran a fingertip around
the rim of her glass. Everything about the man was intriguing, that was the problem!

Swallowing the last of her iced tea, Ellen pushed back
her chair. "I'd better go. I promised Sammy I'd only be
a few minutes." Getting up, she leaned against the table
for a moment, and Capri thought she saw her wince.

"Are you all right, Ellen?" Capri's concerned gaze
encompassed the other woman's face before moving to
the large bulge under her dress...a bulge which seemed
to have dropped considerably in the last couple of days.

Beads of perspiration glistened on the redhead's
freckled brow. "Oh, I'm fine. Just feeling the heat is
all. I'll go lie down for a while..."

She paused on the top step and stooped sideways to
pick up the branch she'd tossed down earlier. Then,

straightening, she pressed one hand against the small of her back and looked in the direction of Taggart's cabin.

"It's too bad the two of you didn't hit it off," she murmured, rubbing the back of her hand against the base of her spine. "When we were standing in the kitchen last night, I couldn't help thinking that the pair of you looked so *right* together—Taggart such a hunk with his blond hair and blue eyes, and you so pretty and dark and fragile-looking." Ellen sighed wistfully. "The way he looked at you when he said you were going to walk along the beach together—it sent shivers down my spine! I was hoping..."

"Ellen, don't waste your time," Capri said briskly. She remembered his look only too well...it had sent shivers down her spine too! But she didn't want to think about that... "I have no intention of becoming involved with Taggart Smith, or anyone else. I meant what I said the other day, about never planning to marry."

"Who's talking about marriage?"

"Well, I'm *certainly* not interested in having an affair!" Capri managed to sound shocked. The last thing she'd want Ellen to guess was how close she might have been to that the previous evening, had Taggart not pulled back.

"An affair with Taggart Smith." There was no mistaking the dreamy note in Ellen's voice. "Oh, Capri, Sammy would kill me if he heard me say this, but...only a *fool* would turn down the chance!"

As the perky redhead ambled away with a rueful wave of her leafy branch, Capri found her own gaze pulled hypnotically toward the line of trees sheltering Taggart's cabin.

No, she reflected tautly, as she stepped back into the kitchen, you're quite wrong, Ellen. I wouldn't be a fool to turn down the chance of having an affair with Taggart Smith.

I'd be a fool not to!

*   *   *

Zoe and Taggart spent the latter part of the morning together on the beach.

The first indication Capri had of their presence was Zoe's throaty laugh. The sound drifted through the open window about half an hour after Ellen's departure, as Capri was washing out her undies in the sink. She took a deep breath, and pulled back the curtains.

The two were strolling from the direction of Taggart's cabin, Zoe in a sleek silver bikini, Taggart in a pair of navy trunks. Zoe's blond hair was loose and it swept in a gleaming swathe down her back, almost to her waist. She ran the fingers of one hand through it in a flirty, feminine way as she looked up at Taggart and said something Capri couldn't hear. He glanced down at her with an indulgent smile on his lean, tanned face... and Capri felt a searing stab of jealousy.

Why did they have to come to this particular section of the beach? she wondered angrily. The sand stretched for half a mile; surely they would have more privacy if they'd walked right to the end... to the sheltered area where she and Taggart had had their row?

With abrupt, irritable movements, she rinsed the suds from her bra and panties and let the water run from the sink, unable to drag her gaze from outside. They made a stunning couple, she thought tightly... both so blond, so tanned, their bodies so magnificently, so perfectly proportioned.

She wanted to turn away, but couldn't. And as she watched, Zoe threw a handful of sand at Taggart, who retaliated by scooping her up in his arms and striding towards the surf. He splashed forward till he was waist-deep, and then tossed her into the water as easily as if she were a Barbie doll, her shrill screams rending the air.

When finally they staggered back up the beach together, they collapsed on the towels Zoe spread out for them. They lay close together, and when Capri saw the blond woman kneel beside Taggart and begin applying suntan lotion to his back, she could stand it no longer. Feeling as if with each stroke Zoe was stabbing a knife into her heart, she withdrew from the window, and stumbled to her bedroom. There she threw herself on the bed, and closed her eyes.

But the tears were not to be confined. They squeezed from behind her eyelids, and rolled down her cheeks. And within minutes her pillow was drenched.

CHAPTER SEVEN

A STORM must be in the offing, Capri decided with an anxious frown as she walked up the beach in mid-afternoon after a refreshing swim. There was a hush in the air, a waiting. Not a bird sang. The sun was a huge burning globe in the blue-gray sky, its heat baking the earth, its hazy rays causing the world to shimmer.

Blotting the salt water from around her eyes with her pink terry towel, she stepped quickly over the burning sand till she reached the grassy slope in front of her cabin. She paused there, and, dropping her head forward so that her hair fell dripping in front of her, she closed her eyes and began to towel it dry. She'd stayed in her cabin all day, to avoid bumping into Taggart, but in the end the heat had got the better of her. Waiting till there was no one around, she had put on her bikini and run down to——

"Apparently there's going to be a storm in the next while. When it breaks, you may need this."

The words, quietly spoken, broke abruptly into Capri's thoughts, and she felt her heart rocket against her chest. Taggart! Where had he come from?

Stealing a moment to gather her composure and steady her pounding pulse, she gave her hair one last brisk rub, before capturing it inside the towel and swathing the pink terry around her head turban-style.

Only then did she turn around.

He was standing right behind her, and when she saw him her throat muscles constricted so forcefully that she was afraid she was going to choke. He was wearing rugged cotton shorts in the same shade of golden-brown as his tanned body, and for a heart-stopping moment she had thought he was naked. Naked, and bronzed by the sun, like some magnificent god.

Blue eyes blank, he held out her navy jacket. The jacket which she'd left on the grass the night before when she'd flung herself up and stormed away from him...

"Oh..." Though her arm felt frozen, she forced herself to reach out and take the jacket. "Thanks."

As she curled her fingers into the pile-lined garment, she noticed his gaze flickering down over her body, and she became uncomfortably aware that she was once again wearing her revealing black bikini. Awkwardly, she clutched the jacket over her breasts. "You're right—if it storms, I'll need this. It's the only rainproof thing I brought with me."

He turned to go.

"Taggart——" She'd blurted out his name before she could stop herself. And immediately she had she wished desperately she could call it back again, but it was too late.

He paused for a beat, and then turned slowly to face her again. "Yes, Capri?"

Capri. It was the first time he'd called her by her first name. She had grown used to his mocking "Jones"... had actually grown to like it. There had always been an edge of affection to it. Dully, Capri realized that by switching to her Christian name he was trying to tell her something—but what? That he no longer got any fun out of teasing her? That he had been turned off by her anger the night before? By her rejection of him? By her horridly snide comment about Zoe? "Nothing," she said in a flat little voice. "Just...thanks for bringing back my jacket."

"No problem." His eyebrow rose inquiringly. "That's it?"

Capri hesitated. She *could* apologize, of course... but some deep instinct told her that it was too late...the damage had been done and it was irreparable. "The storm——" she gestured toward the sky "—what can I expect?"

"You haven't been listening to the radio?"

"I didn't bring one to the island with me." She looked up at him, but avoided meeting his eyes; instead she fixed her own on a spot just above his left brow. "I didn't expect I'd need one—and, as you know," she said thinly, "I came here for peace and quiet."

"There should be a battery radio in your cabin——"

"If there is, I haven't seen it."

She saw his jaw tighten. "It'll be there, somewhere."

Abruptly he turned away again, but instead of going in the direction of his own cabin as she expected he began striding toward hers. She hesitated for just a moment, and then hurried after him.

"They're forecasting hurricane-force winds." The clipped words came back to Capri over his broad shoulder. "They're expected to reach a hundred and twenty kilometres an hour, and they'll probably hit here sometime around midnight."

Capri didn't catch up with him till they were both in the kitchen. Tossing her jacket over the back of a chair, she said breathlessly, "If there *is* a radio, it isn't in the kitchen. I'd have come across it by now——"

"Probably in here, then." Without waiting for a response, he strode through to the bedroom. There was a cupboard behind the door, and Capri had briefly examined the contents shortly after her arrival. It had contained extra blankets, some paperback books, an assortment of jars and vases, and a couple of life-jackets. Now, as Taggart swung the door open, the first thing she noticed was a small white transistor radio, tucked neatly in between two stacks of books on the bottom shelf.

"Oh," she murmured with an apologetic grimace, "there it is." Automatically, she crouched down to reach for it . . . but Taggart apparently had the same idea. They bumped into each other, Capri's silky-smooth arm sliding against his muscled shoulder. She jerked back and straightened to her feet as if she'd been scalded. "Sorry," she muttered, painfully aware of the flood of color to her cheeks.

"That's all right." His words were steady, his voice as calm as if nothing had happened. Extricating the radio, he stood up and switched it on. The volume control must have been set on high, for suddenly music thundered into the small room with an unexpectedness that set Capri's nerves jumping.

Taggart turned the volume down. "Battery appears to be all right——"

He broke off, and Capri saw him stiffen as his gaze lit on the photo of Jamie perched on her bedside table. He was close enough that he would have no trouble reading the inscription—and as he stared openly at her brother's laughing, handsome face she could almost hear the words echoing in the air between them . . . "To my other half."

Taggart would, she guessed, be recalling how she'd used those exact same words when he'd coaxed her into telling him how she'd been hurt at one time. And surely he would be assuming—because she'd kept this photo and carried it around—that though she'd been hurt she still loved the man who had been responsible for her pain. And he'd be right, she thought wearily . . .

She expected Taggart to pass some comment, but he didn't. Instead, he turned his head and looked at her for a second, his eyes strangely hooded, and then he sidestepped her and went through to the kitchen. "You'll be able to listen for the weather reports," he said as she followed him, "and keep up-to-date with what's happening. I'll find the right station for you before I go." His voice was as devoid of emotion as a recorded message coming across a telephone line.

How could he do it? Capri wondered bewilderedly. How could he block off the rapport they'd developed...not to mention all the electricity that had been jumping between them till last night? Her own body was a seething mass of longings—longing to touch him, longing to wipe the distant expression from his face, longing to hear once again his teasingly drawled, "Hey, Jones."

With a distracted exclamation, she took a corner of the towel which had slipped from her pink turban and poked it back into place again under her left ear. What was the matter with her? She'd never felt this way before about a man... miserable and confused and desperately longing for just one smile from him... She was acting like a love-sick teenager...

Shock jolted through her so powerfully she felt herself sway. Wide-eyed, she stared at Taggart as—oblivious to her stunned state—he concentrated on turning the tuning dial on the radio. And, as she looked at him, an overwhelming tenderness spilled over inside her, filling every last little corner of her body with the warmth and exquisite sweetness of melted honey. As if for the first time, she saw the crinkles fanning from the corners of his eyes, the firm, resolute set of his wide, sensual mouth, the strong planes of his jaw. What a very beautiful man he was, she thought—physically, mentally, and every other way she could think of.

She realized she was holding her breath, and as she exhaled silently she had a vivid picture of her heart—not the way it really was, but transformed into a masterpiece of padded red satin like a heart on a Valentine card. It was pierced in the center by a silver arrow, sharp and straight and true...and the inscription she could see on it drained the last of the strength from her bones:

Capri Jones loves Taggart Smith.

She leaned back against the countertop, hardly aware of the hard Formica edge jutting into her back as Taggart clicked the radio off and set it on the table.

"That's it," he said brusquely. "I'll be off now."

Dazedly, Capri looked at him, not answering. He looked around at her, lines of irritation drawing his brows together, and Capri gripped the edge of the countertop as she waited for him to leave.

But he wasn't ready to go. "What's the matter?" he asked in a curt tone. "You look as if you've just seen a ghost."

A ghost? Capri felt her heart contract with pain. Yes, she had just seen a ghost. As she had faced the devastating discovery that she had fallen in love with Taggart Smith, she had seen Jamie's ghost. And as her brother's image had drifted before her eyes it had been accompanied by the poignant reminder of just how much pain his loss had caused her.

She had promised herself she would never risk her heart again. Now she realized with a feeling of agony how very careless she had been . . .

"It's the heat," she said, hoping her excuse would explain the tremor in her voice. "It's given me a slight headache. A couple of aspirin and I'll be all right again."

He nodded abruptly. "Good. Remember, if you need anything . . ."

Capri waited, her nerves stretched to breaking-point. Was he going to tell her to come to him? But she couldn't do that . . . not now . . . now knowing how she felt about him. She would have to keep away from him, and not allow herself to become even more entangled than she already was. "Yes?"

". . . you'll find Zoe very helpful."

As he turned away, Capri could see sweat glistening on his back, on his arms, on the hair covering his hard thighs. And she noticed that where he stepped his bare feet left very faint damp imprints on the linoleum-covered floor.

He swung the door lightly closed behind him, and as soon as he'd gone Capri stumbled to the window. Fingers clutching the plastic curtains, she stared, mesmerized, as—arrogant, distant, forbidding—he strode down the beach and out to the end of the jetty.

When he got there, he stood there for a long moment, and seemed to be staring out to sea, his magnificent body a dark outline against the clear blue sky. Then he dived into the water, and was lost to Capri's view beyond the narrow wooden structure.

As she turned from the window she hunched over, and hugged her arms around herself, the way she did when she had a stomachache. But the ache wasn't in her stomach; the ache was in her heart.

And she knew that the longer she stayed, and the more she saw of Taggart, the more unbearable that ache was going to become.

She had to get away. She had to protect herself. But she didn't want Taggart to guess she was leaving because of him—it would be too humiliating—so she wouldn't leave right away.

She would wait till after the storm.

"A storm warning is in effect for Vancouver Island, and the west coast of British Columbia. Gale-force winds are expected around midnight tonight, gusting up to one hundred and twenty kilometres per hour..."

Capri switched off the weather forecast which had followed the six o'clock news, and, leaning back in her patio lounger, closed her eyes. Though the sticky heat had taken away her appetite, she had made herself a small mushroom omelett for dinner, and had sat outside in the shade at the back of the cabin to pick at it. But even here, because there wasn't even the hint of a breeze from the ocean, she was finding it unbearably muggy.

Now, with the weatherman's words of warning still ringing in her ears, she sipped from a glass of chilled lemonade and found her thoughts drawn to Taggart...as they had been all day.

Was it really possible to fall in love with someone in less than a week? *Was* it love, or just infatuation? No, she decided miserably, it wasn't infatuation. What she felt for Taggart was no foolish passion based solely on physical attraction. Oh, it might have started that way— from the moment she'd set eyes on him she'd been incredibly attracted to him sexually—but as she'd grown to know him she'd begun to feel a strong bond between them, a bond of mutual compassion and warmth. She liked him. She liked everything about him. She liked his sense of humor, his gentleness with Miranda, his kindness to Ellen. She also liked his practicality—the way he'd swept her hair so swiftly from the flames of the lamp, the way he wielded his tongs over the barbecue coals, the way he'd packed Ellen off to bed when she wasn't feeling well. Her lips twisted wryly. The list of things she liked about him went on forever——

The heavy thud of feet on the ground at the front of her cabin startled her, and, laying down her glass, she jumped up. And as she rounded the corner to investigate, Sam whirled into view, skidding to a halt when he saw her. His normally neat hair was disheveled, his face ashen.

Capri felt a shiver of apprehension run down her spine. "What's the matter, Sam?" she asked urgently. "What's happened?"

He groaned. "Oh, God, Capri—it's Miranda. She fell outside the cabin and gashed her lip on a tree stump. It's a bad cut. There was blood everywhere—I thought she was going to pass out—and Ellen was frantic—I thought she was going to pass out too! We've managed to stop the bleeding—I'm surprised you didn't hear her screaming——"

"Oh, damn! I had the radio on. Sam, is there anything I can do?"

"I'm looking for Taggart—he's not in his cabin and I hoped he might be here. I want to take Miranda to the mainland—right away. She's going to need stitches——"

"I haven't seen him since the middle of the afternoon—he went for a swim——" As Capri spoke, she looked around distractedly, and her attention was caught by a movement in the distance. She heaved a sigh of relief—and at the same time felt a razor-sharp twinge of jealousy. Taggart and Zoe had appeared halfway along the beach, and were walking toward them. Zoe was hanging on to Taggart's arm.

Capri forced herself to concentrate on the problem at hand and not allow herself to wonder where the two had been...and what they had been doing. "There he is, Sam."

Sam whirled around. "Oh, thank the Lord." He mopped the sweat from his brow with his shirt sleeve. "Capri, would you go and tell him what's happened? Ask if I can take one of the boats—I'll go back to the cabin and get Miranda——"

"Is Ellen all right?" Capri called back over her shoulder as, kicking off her sandals, she began running.

"She's absolutely done in, first with the heat, then with the worry over Miranda. She's going to lie down." Sam took off around the corner of the cabin, and once more Capri heard his feet thudding on the ground as he ran back to get his daughter.

Poor little Miranda! Capri felt her heart go out to the toddler. With fleeting steps she raced along the beach, the soles of her feet barely skimming the burning hot sand. "Hoy," she shouted, "Taggart!" Wildly she waved to him, and when he noticed her at last he said something to Zoe, and the two of them broke into a run, moving swiftly in her direction.

When they met, Capri said breathlessly, "It's Miranda, Taggart. She's cut her lip quite badly and it needs stitches. Sam wants to take her to the mainland——"

Zoe said, "I'll take them over, Tag. In the *Pretty Polly.*"

Taggart muttered a soft curse. "Poor kid...yes, of course you must take them to the mainland, but..." He raised a hand to shade his eyes as he peered at the distant horizon, and then he shook his head. "I don't like it, Zoe. When that storm comes, it's going to be a bad one. You'll get there before it breaks, there's no doubt about that, but... Take the *Blueberry Blazer*—it's faster. And the three of you will have to stay in Vancouver overnight. By the time Miranda is seen to it'll be far too late to risk the trip back."

They had been walking quickly along the beach as they talked, and by the time they were below Capri's cabin they saw Sam striding down the hill toward them with Miranda in his arms. Both were wearing orange life jackets.

"How is she?" Taggart's tone was taut.

"Sleepy, thank heavens." Sam had a knapsack slung over his shoulder. "I've got our overnight things. We'll stay till tomorrow, Taggart——"

"Yes. And Zoe will take you over."

"She will?" Sam's eyes shone with relief. "That'll make things a lot easier. Thanks a million, Taggart. How can I ever repay you for all——?"

"Get along, Sam." There was an impatient note in Taggart's voice. "Zoe, do you need to get anything from your cabin?"

The caretaker shook her head as she slapped the hip pocket of her jeans. "My wallet's here... I'll stay at my cousin's place in Vancouver and we can get in touch tomorrow morning, Sam, and make our plans for coming back."

Capri got a brief glimpse of Miranda's face as Sam carried her into the boat and she felt her heart clench. She couldn't see the toddler's mouth, as it was concealed by a loose gauze pad, but her freckled skin looked dreadfully pale, and her carroty curls lay in damp bedragglement over her brow. There was a smear of dried blood on her cheek.

As Zoe put on her life jacket, Sam murmured something to Taggart—Capri thought she heard Ellen's name mentioned, and she saw Taggart frown, but couldn't hear his reply. Moments later, the caretaker started the engine, and it throbbed steadily in the stillness of the afternoon. Capri and Taggart stood without talking as it drew away from the jetty. They were quite close, and Capri couldn't avoid inhaling the sweaty male scent of him. It was a heady essence, so familiar already, so utterly, so compellingly seductive that she couldn't bear it. Tears stung her eyes as she turned and started walking away.

Before she'd taken half a dozen steps, she heard Taggart's voice.

"Radio working all right?"

She blinked back the evidence of her distress before turning to look at him. "Yes, thanks," she answered, cursing the unsteadiness of her tone. "It's Okay. I listened to the weather forecast a little while ago." She hesitated. His expression was drawn, fatigued, and instantly she forgot all her own unhappiness. "Don't worry," she offered impulsively. "Miranda's going to be all right, and they're going to get to the mainland long before the storm starts."

He glanced at the square gold watch at his wrist. "Oh, yes, I'm sure they'll make it in good time. If I'd had any doubts, I wouldn't have allowed them to go."

"What's the matter, then?"

He looked as if he was about to say something, but then changed his mind. Shaking his head, he said curtly,

"Nothing you need to worry your pretty little head about."

Capri's concern for him dissipated instantaneously, to be replaced by a spurt of anger. Certainly she had been dreadfully rude and insulting the night before, but did she really deserve this frigid treatment? "Fine," she snapped. "Then we can each go our separate ways again." She pivoted on her bare heel and marched away from him, up the path to her cabin, her chin tilted haughtily in the air.

How could you be in love with a man, she wondered as she slammed the door shut behind her with a resounding bang, and still want to throttle him?

Her report was finished.

Capri sat back in her chair, feeling a great sense of satisfaction. She had set out the problem, and had come up with several possible solutions. The first was the onsite day care she'd considered earlier. The second was to approach other companies in the immediate area of the Jones Oil building to see if they were interested in purchasing a property and developing a common facility; the third to provide subsidies where economically necessary so mothers could afford better quality day care; the fourth to form a committee to do a study of existing day care facilities in the area, and, where the committee approved, reserve a permanent number of places for company employees; and the fifth to provide a day care referral service for employees.

She hoped the board would approve. She was convinced that, if they accepted some or all of her recommendations not only would it alleviate the absenteeism, it would make life much less stressful for the female employees at Jones Oil.

Rubbing her nape to relieve the tension that had gathered there, she packed her computer into its case, and gathered all her files neatly together. And as she glanced out of the window she saw that it was going to be dark soon.

There was a strange, eerie feeling in the air, and the sky had a hazy pink tinge. The sea was like glass, the grass limp and still.

The storm was biding its time. Like a formidable actor waiting unseen in the wings, letting the tension build— knowing that when he swept on stage the waiting would be forgotten.

She longed for it to be over.

For, after the storm, she would go home.

CHAPTER EIGHT

AN ALMIGHTY crack of thunder reverberated across the heavens, shattering Capri's dreams and jerking her awake. She sat bolt upright in the pitch darkness, her heart thudding, and realized that the room was freezing cold. When she'd turned in around ten-thirty, it had been warm outside, so she had left the window open. Now she could feel a chilly draught, hear the cotton curtains flapping wildly against the bedroom wall.

She slid from her bed, and, groping in the inky blackness for her robe, pulled it over her silk nightshirt and scrambled to the window. Just as she reached it, there was a blinding flash of lightning, and the scene outside was starkly illuminated, as if by a powerful flare.

She stared, hypnotized by the eerie bone-whiteness of the beach, the jetty, the wildly heaving ocean...and then the lightning faded and everything was shrouded again in black. For a long moment she stood tensely, hearing nothing but the howling of the wind, a wailing sound that chilled her blood. But as she listened, something cold and wet slapped her cheeks, and, gasping, she realized that rain had started to fall, and the gale was whipping it through the open window.

She fumbled for the sash and banged it shut, shivering as another peal of thunder rolled across the heavens. A glance at the illuminated face of her watch showed her it was just a minute after three. The storm had arrived slightly later than scheduled; Sam, Miranda, and Zoe would have been safely in Vancouver hours ago.

But how would Ellen be coping with being alone?

Capri nibbled her lip anxiously, hardly hearing the deafening tattoo above her as a torrential deluge pounded the corrugated tin roof of the cabin. She had gone to check on the other woman around eight, and had found her scrubbing the kitchen floor, her face dripping with perspiration.

"For heaven's sake, Ellen," she'd cried out, "what are you *doing*? I thought Sam ordered you to stay in bed!"

"It's all right, Capri—I feel much better now. I want the place to look bright and shiny for Sam and——"

"You're going to knock yourself out, that's what you're going to do! Now you sit down, and I'll finish the floor."

But Ellen had insisted on finishing the job herself. Capri had stayed till around ten, and as she left Ellen had said teasingly, "Be sure to batten down before the storm..."

Now Capri uttered a frustrated exclamation as she listened to the screaming gale. Would Ellen be awake? How could she not be? she thought, as thunder roared again across the heavens—and it wouldn't be good for her...or her unborn baby...if she were to be upset by the storm.

Capri sighed. She could stay here and worry...or she could go see if Ellen needed company. She knew in her heart that she wouldn't be able to relax till she found out if the perky redhead was all right.

Ten minutes later, dressed in jeans, sweatshirt, and jacket—with the hood on and snugly tied at the neck— she opened her outside door. She gasped as the gale tried to snatch it from her, and, gritting her teeth, she braced herself against the wind and forced the door shut again.

By the time she'd climbed the hill and reached the other cabin she felt as if all the breath had been battered from her body. The wind had torn the hood back from her head, her hair was plastered over her brow, and her jeans felt like a cold, wet second skin. But when she saw light glowing dimly from the kitchen window she was glad she had come.

But no matter how hard she knocked, no one answered, and Capri surmised that if Ellen did hear the banging she would attribute it to the furor of the storm. Finally, after testing the door handle, and finding it giving under her touch, she entered the kitchen in a flurry of wind and rain.

For a moment she leaned back against the door, panting, rain streaming down her face and dripping from the tip of her nose.

And then she heard it... a sound from the bedroom.

She froze... but only for a fraction of a second... Then, without waiting to take off her saturated jacket, she hurried across the kitchen. As she reached the doorway leading to the bedroom she came to a dead stop. A lantern sat on the bedside table, casting a golden glow over the room—and over Ellen, who was lying on her side on the double bed. Her eyes were screwed tightly shut, her pointed features twisted in agony as she writhed under the covers.

Capri steadied herself against the doorjamb as the groans slowly faded away. Dear God, she thought in horror, what's happening?

Ellen's eyes flew open, and Capri realized she must have spoken her thoughts aloud. She saw relief flicker across the other woman's face. "Capri... oh, it's good to see you." A freckled hand was held out in weary greeting. "Did Taggart tell you to come?"

"Taggart?" Capri peeled off her waterlogged jacket and, without taking her gaze from Ellen, tossed it down behind the door. "No, I haven't seen him. I came because I was worried about you——"

"So did Taggart." Ellen made an attempt at a smile, but it didn't quite come off. She dropped her hand limply on the bedcover. "I had a few cramps this morning and when they passed I thought they must have been caused by something I ate—but Sam obviously thought it might be something more and he was worried. He asked Taggart to keep an eye on me. He came just before you did.''

So that was what Sam had been saying to Taggart before he left with Miranda for the mainland! Capri glanced around sharply. ''Where *is* Taggart?''

''He's gone to contact a friend who owns a helicopter company near Vancouver airport—he's going to ask if he can send a chopper to take me to hospital. He's going to try to contact my doctor too, and get some instructions.''

''Instructions?'' Capri moved dazedly to the bed.

''For delivering my baby, in case...'' Before she could say any more, Ellen's face creased again in pain, and once again Capri heard the wild groaning.

Disbelievingly, Capri looked at the thin contorted face. Ellen was in labor...and even with the limited knowledge Capri had she was in no doubt that that labor was well advanced. She felt her legs tremble...

Ellen's freckled hands clutched convulsively for the edge of her bedcover, and, hardly aware of what she was doing, Capri reached out for them and grasped them with her own. The other woman squeezed them so tightly that Capri found herself wincing. Who would have thought someone so slight would have so much strength?

As the groans began to die away again, Ellen nodded weakly toward a plastic bowl of water that was lying on the bedside table, a floral washcloth floating on the surface. ''Capri, my face is so hot—would you mind...?''

Capri wrung out the cloth, and gently sponged Ellen's brow. ''The contractions, Ellen...when did they begin again? And why didn't you let anyone know?''

Ellen closed her eyes. ''They started again around midnight, but, like earlier in the day, they weren't bad...just slight twinges. I thought they might pass...and then they didn't. I thought I'd probably have a long labor like last time, so I was going to wait till morning to ask Taggart to arrange transportation for me—then things started happening so fast——"

The sound of the outside door crashing open, and shutting again violently, broke into Ellen's words. It could only be Taggart, Capri thought. She forced herself not to look around; forced herself to go on applying the cool damp cloth soothingly over Ellen's pale cheeks.

"Ellen, I'm back. How's it going?" Taggart swept across the kitchen with the force of a tornado, but his heavy footsteps stopped short as he came through the doorway of the bedroom. "How did *you* get here?" he demanded bluntly.

Capri knew he must be addressing her. Without raising her eyes, she said as calmly as she could, "The same way as you, probably...blown by the gale!"

"Taggart," Ellen's voice was thin, "did you talk with your friend?"

Surreptitiously Capri watched Taggart approach the bed. He was wearing a navy coat that streamed with rain, and his thick blond hair looked as if it was painted to his head, showing off the beautifully symmetrical shape of his skull. He looked more rugged than ever, with his face wet and the best part of a day's stubble bristling his jaw. Concerned though she was for Ellen, Capri couldn't help noticing how just the sight of him was making her heart flip around like a fish caught in a net.

"I did get hold of Brock." Taggart's brows gathered in a frown. "He was reluctant to send any of his pilots out in a storm like this...he's going to come himself. Damned wind," he muttered, almost to himself. "It's so strong, and visibility's nil, but..." He blew out a sigh, and smiled to Ellen, but Capri could see that the smile didn't reach his eyes. "Don't worry, Ellen. Everything's going to be just fine."

"Thanks so much, Taggart." Ellen's lips looked dry, and she licked them with the tip of her tongue.

"I talked with Dr. Haffey, too." Taggart's voice was reassuring.

"You did?"

"He's told me what to do...in case the chopper doesn't get here in time——"

Taggart stopped talking as a roll of thunder drowned out his words, and, before he could continue, Ellen muttered, "Oh, God, here it goes again..."

Her whole body tensed, and she flung out her hands with a hoarse cry. Capri forced herself to act; dropping the washcloth back in the basin of water, she grasped the clutching fingers, trying to send encouragement to her by the firmness of her own grip.

"Have you any experience of...of this type of situation?" Taggart's voice was low and intense, and Capri realized he was talking to her.

"No," she said quietly, and for the first time looked directly up at him. "I don't."

"I want to get the wood stove going." His features were taut. "The kitchen window was wide open when I got here—the whole place is like an icebox."

Capri glanced at Ellen, and noted she had relaxed again. Amazingly, she seemed to be asleep. "What else did the doctor say?" Capri whispered.

"That Ellen's pregnancy had been normal," he said tersely, "and that he expected the delivery to be without complications. He was surprised that she'd gone into labor early, but when he saw Miranda last evening——"

"Oh, is she all right?"

"Fine. She needed several stitches, but the scar should be minimal. Haffey felt the shock of the accident was probably what triggered Ellen's labor."

"Sam told her to rest...but I found her scrubbing the kitchen floor after he left," Capri murmured.

"I think that's common—nature's way of ensuring the mother has a nice clean nest for the new born." Taggart shrugged his broad shoulders out of his jacket, revealing a navy crew-necked sweater and a pair of jeans that were soaked from the thighs down. His running shoes—like her own—were dripping wet, Capri noticed, and he was wearing no socks. "Can you manage without the lamp till I get the fire going?"

Capri bit her lip as she glanced at Ellen's sweat-beaded face. "I...I...think so..."

"Good." Swinging up the lantern from the bedside table, he disappeared into the kitchen, leaving the bedroom in dusky shadows.

Capri alternately consoled and encouraged Ellen, and in the quieter moments when there was a lull between the tension of the contractions, and the gusts of wind and thunderclaps, she could hear Taggart rummaging about in the kitchen, setting the fire and getting it going. Afterward, she heard him pump water, imagined him washing his hands.

The flickering of the shadows on the bedroom wall alerted her to his return. As he put the lantern back on the bedside table, Capri noticed that he had also brought with him a neatly folded white sheet, several white towels, one of Miranda's soft blankets, and a box of tissues.

"Taggart..." Ellen's voice wavered between them. "You'll need a diaper for the baby. In the dresser, in the bottom drawer, you'll find a few cloth ones. I use them for Miranda...at bedtime. They'll be too big, of course, but there's a pair of scissors in the top drawer—you can cut one down..."

Capri watched Taggart as he moved over to the dresser. Watched as he carefully did as Ellen had suggested. How capable he was, how calm, and self-assured. As strong and dependable as a rock. Love swelled up inside her with a power that rocked her to the core.

As Ellen was trapped by another contraction, one that seemed much stronger than any that had gone before, he touched Capri on the shoulder to attract her attention.

"How long between each contraction now?"

"There's very little space between them at all," she replied quickly. Before she could say more, Ellen let out a scream. And as she screamed she flailed out wildly with her arms, almost hitting Capri, who had bent forward anxiously.

"It's coming," Ellen squealed. "It's coming."

"Capri," Taggart grasped her shoulders roughly and turned her in the direction of the kitchen, "go and wash your hands. *Scrub them*. And hop to it. I'm going to need you here."

Capri felt her mouth go dry. "What...what for?"

"You and I," he replied with a grim twist of his lips, "are about to bring a baby into the world."

Taggart had obviously listened well to Dr. Haffey's instructions, for he commanded the operation as if he'd been delivering babies all his life...

While Ellen groaned and cried out, he moved into action.

"She should be lying on her back now—Capri, help me turn her over. See if there's an extra pillow in the closet..."

She hurried across the room and wrenched the door open. "There are two, Taggart——"

"Put them both under her head. Good. Now, take the bedcover off, drape her with this sheet."

"Taggart," Capri's voice was soft with awe, "I can see the baby's crown..."

"Ellen," Taggart's voice rose urgently, "don't push. Hold back..."

For the next few minutes, Capri watched, utterly stunned, as Taggart guided Ellen into her delivery. Watched, barely breathing, as the baby's head began to appear, supported by Taggart's palms...

"That's good, Ellen, the head's turning nicely, oh, that's great, you're doing so well... It'll be all over soon..."

Then at last, when the head had emerged completely and was tenderly cupped in Taggart's hands, Ellen gave a tremendous push and the baby slipped into the world, its tiny body looking frail and precious on the towel Taggart had spread out to receive it.

"It's a boy, Ellen!" Taggart's voice was as elated, as triumphant, Capri thought with a tremulous smile, as if the child were his own.

Ellen raised her head from the pillows, her neck muscles taut. Her hair was soaked with sweat, her face ethereally pale. "Is he all right?" Though her voice was barely audible, there was no doubt about her anxiety.

"He's perfect," Taggart said gruffly...

The next moments passed in a blur. Capri helped while Taggart expertly tilted the little body to clear the fluid in the nose and throat; she wiped the puckish face with one of the tissues as he directed her; she felt a thrill of elation when the baby let out his first, lusty yell; and she watched with wonder as the expanding of his lungs quickly turned his face bright pink.

Taggart held the slippery body while she dried it gently with a warm towel, and together they tucked him into the nappy, and wrapped him in Miranda's cozy cream blanket.

Then, with a tenderness in his movements that spoke more than any words, Taggart held out the little bundle for its mother to inspect.

"Oh, Taggart..." Tears shone in Ellen's green eyes. "He's absolutely beautiful. And so like Sam."

Capri felt tears choking her own throat as she looked on. Seeing Taggart with a baby in his arms made her feel as if she was melting with love for him, but as Ellen gazed adoringly at the fragile bundle cradled gently in his arms, wonder in her expression, incredulity in her eyes as she touched the tiny fingers, Capri found the picture almost unbearably moving. With her own decision not to marry, not to have children, she had never realized just how much she was giving up. It now hit her with a terrible force, the enormity of what she was going to miss out on. It was something truly awesome . . . a miracle . . .

Ellen sighed happily and let her head fall back on the pillows. "He'll be Samuel, like his father. And we'll call him Samuel, not Sammy, to distinguish them . . ."

Drained of energy and with a shine of joy in her eyes—eyes which were also glazed with shock following the trauma of delivery—Ellen seemed oblivious to everything but her new baby as Taggart laid the compact bundle on its side in her arms.

"Capri . . ."

"Yes?" Capri dragged her rapt gaze from the mother and child as Taggart spoke to her. His eyes were fixed on the baby, and she felt shock and horror jolt through her as she saw how haggard he looked, how ashen his face beneath his tan.

"I can deal with the rest." His voice was low but harsh. "How about making us all a good strong pot of tea?"

"Sounds good," she managed, her deliberately light tone belying her anxiety. *What was wrong with him?* A moment ago, he'd been elated . . . now his eyes were dark and tormented, his jaw tightly clamped as if he was afraid of what he might say. She had to fight an almost overwhelming urge to cry out, to reach over with her fingertips and smooth away the grim, hard lines etched around his mouth—to plead with him to tell her what was causing him such anguish . . .

Instead, she made a pretense of adjusting the sleeves of her sweatshirt, which she'd rolled up earlier. "It's nice and warm in here now," she murmured. "But the fire may be dying down a little by now. Should I stoke it up?"

"If you would." He didn't look at her as he answered.

Capri began walking across the room, but, to her dismay, found her legs wobbling as if they were made of rubber.

She leaned against the sink for support as she pumped the water to start it running into the kettle, unable to stop thinking about the sudden drastic change in Taggart's attitude. While he'd been delivering the baby, he'd been warm, and tender, and kind; now that it was all over he seemed to have slipped away, leaving a Taggart Smith she didn't recognize.

Did it have something to do with her? Instinctively she knew it didn't. But if not her, then what—or whom? Ellen? The baby?

She shook her head despairingly as, forcing herself to move, she rummaged in the cupboard for teabags. When she had first met him, on that sunny afternoon which now seemed aeons ago, she had thought him a simple man. How very wrong she had been!

If he had seemed simple, it was only on the surface. She had had the opportunity to see just a little way below that surface, but it was enough to let her know that Taggart Smith was the most complex, deep, and puzzling person she had ever met.

She stood alone on the beach, huddled in her wet jacket, as Ellen was carried on a stretcher to the helicopter.

Taggart's pilot friend Brock, along with a paramedic, had arrived as dawn was breaking, and now, as a watery sun slid higher into the sulky sky, they were about to take the new mother and baby to the hospital on the mainland.

The worst of the storm had passed over, though the wind still gusted a little. It fluffed through Ellen's gingery curls as, cocooned in a heavy wool blanket and with baby Samuel warmly folded in her arms, she lifted her head from the stretcher. "Goodbye, Capri," she called gaily. "Give Taggart your address. I want to write to you..."

Unable to speak for the emotion blocking her throat, Capri raised a hand in farewell. Taggart had managed to contact Sam, and he and Miranda were to be waiting at the hospital for Ellen. How she wished she could be there, to see the joyful reunion.

As the door of the chopper slammed shut, Capri turned away. She felt her heart twisting bleakly. Sam, Ellen, their little girl, their little boy. A perfect, happy family unit. She herself had once been part of such a unit, a unit comprising her father, her mother, Jamie, and herself. Her mother's face, at one time, must have glowed with happiness, the way Ellen's did today. Her mother, too, must have looked forward with eagerness to the years they would all spend together.

Why did life hold out such promises, she wondered bitterly, promises it so often didn't keep——?

She started and swiveled around as she heard a sound right behind her, but it wasn't Taggart, as she'd hoped for a fleeting moment. It must have been the wind catching one of the branches that had been whipped on to the beach from the trees during the storm.

She could see him, though—he was walking away toward his cabin, his coat open and flapping in the breeze. She felt pain stabbing through her. With a man like him a woman would be safe, protected. But he didn't want anything to do with her. Not after the way she had rejected him. Not after the spiteful way she'd talked about Zoe.

Dragging her feet, she trudged up the steps to her cabin, her teeth chattering. She would put a fire on and dry out her things. Then she'd start packing. Later on in the day, when Zoe returned to the island, she'd ask the caretaker to take her to Horseshoe Bay. There was nothing left here for her but unhappiness.

Within half an hour she had the cabin toasty warm, and had finally stopped shivering. After making a pot of coffee and washing her hair, she took one of the huge cushions from the living-room, and set it down on the floor in front of the Franklin stove. With her white robe tied tightly around her and a pair of warm pink socks on her feet, she knelt on the cushion, brushing her hair till it was dry and shining, and occasionally sipping from her mug of coffee.

She had just got up to pour herself a second cup and was on her way back to the stove when someone knocked on the door.

She stiffened, spilling a few drops on her wrist. They stung, but she brushed them off distractedly. Who could it be? Surely not Taggart...?

She laid the mug on the countertop. Drawing in an apprehensive breath, she crossed to the door and pulled it open, shivering a little in the chill morning air.

He stood on the doorstep, his face drawn and pale. He was wearing no jacket... just a teal-blue sweater and a pair of black cords... and on his feet the inevitable Reeboks, and no socks. Though his hair was disheveled, as if he'd been running his fingers through it, he had shaved—but carelessly, Capri noted absently, as she saw a fleck of blood on his jaw.

"May I come in?"

May I come in? Capri could hardly believe her ears! Where was the arrogant self-assurance she'd come to expect from this man?

She gestured wordlessly for him to enter, and stepped back as he walked past her, bringing the scents of the island with him. The sky was washed with gray—the whole world seemed gray, she thought unhappily as she pulled the door shut.

Her socks made a scuffling sound on the lino as she padded to the stove and stood with her back to it. She could feel her fingers trembling, and she stuffed them into the patch pockets of her robe to hide them. He had never looked so handsome, so rugged...so very dear. An enormous lump rose in her throat, and with a great effort she managed to swallow it. I love you, she yearned to whisper, I love you.

"What do you want?" Nervousness made her voice sharp.

His blue eyes were dark, the pupils huge. "I came to thank you for helping out with Ellen."

"Oh." Capri chastised herself for the disappointment that stabbed her heart. What had she expected? That he had come to sweep her away to some wonderful paradise on a white charger? "I was glad to be there." And I thought you were too, she wanted to say. And she wanted to ask him why he had seemed so tormented afterward, so...so *haunted*. But instead, all she said in a quiet voice was, "You did a splendid job, Taggart."

He didn't seem to be listening to her. "Coffee smells good." He looked around vaguely.

"Would you like a cup?"

"Mm. Thanks." He moved over to the table, stiffly, as if he were cold, and sat down on one of the chairs.

Capri took another mug from the cupboard, and, as she poured coffee into it, said over her shoulder in a purposefully cheerful voice, "You take sugar, don't you, but no cream?"

There was no answer, just a choking sound, and, turning around with a frown, Capri felt her body freeze. Taggart had his elbows on the table, and his head was in his hands, with the heels of his palms pressed against his eyes. She stared disbelievingly as she heard the small choking sound again.

The sugar bowl slid from Capri's grasp, toppling on to the countertop and spilling some of its contents. She barely noticed. Crossing the space between them in a flash, she knelt down beside Taggart's chair, and tried to pull his hands down from his face. "What's wrong?"

she pleaded. "For pity's sake, Taggart, tell me what's wrong?"

"I'm sorry," he said in a thick, muffled voice. "I'm sorry. I shouldn't have come...but I needed someone to talk to..."

Slowly, Capri let go of him. Feeling as if she were walking on eggshells, she went to sit down on the other chair, not removing her gaze from the slumped figure for even an instant.

"I'm here, Taggart," she said quietly. "Talk to me."

CHAPTER NINE

PAINFULLY slowly, Taggart dragged his hands from his face and even more slowly raised his head.

Capri almost cried out when she saw the tears glazing his eyes, the harsh grooves lining his cheeks. Who—or what—had done this to the laughing, teasing man she loved? She took in a deep breath as she tried to calm herself. "Has it got something to do with Ellen?" she whispered. "With the baby?"

"In a way..." His voice was threaded with pain.

Capri felt a sudden surge of alarm. "There's nothing wrong with little Samuel, is there? You weren't hiding something from Ellen?"

He closed his eyes for a moment, wearily. "Oh, Lord, no. It's nothing like that... If it has anything to with Ellen and the baby it's only indirectly."

"I don't understand..."

"How could you?" His words had a leaden quality. "I'm not making much sense." He pushed his chair back. "I'll begin again, at the beginning...but first, I think I'll have that cup of coffee. No——" he stopped her with a shake of his head as she made to get up "—no, I'll get it."

Instinctively, Capri knew he needed this time to gather himself together.

She watched, her mind whirling with questions, as he mopped up the spilled sugar and filled a mug with coffee. The sound of the teaspoon against the heavy china as he stirred the hot sweet brew echoed in the small room.

"There you go." He placed her mug in front of her, and, cradling his own in his hands, began restlessly pacing the kitchen. "I'm sorry for subjecting you to that display of weakness." His eyes were grim. "I know that nowadays it's supposed to be okay for men to cry—it's even encouraged. But when you've been taught from the time of your first scraped knee that brave boys don't cry it's a hard habit to break."

"Yes," Capri heard a catch in her voice, "yes, I guess it is."

"You remember that morning we had coffee at the Walterses'?"

Capri nodded. "Of course."

"We talked about babies...and families..."

"Yes, I remember." She frowned, recalling the tension that had shimmered between herself and Taggart as the conversation had developed. "Miranda said something to you about babies, and you said you weren't a family man. You laughed, but I couldn't help noticing you seemed...upset."

"You're a very observant woman." Taggart swallowed a mouthful of his coffee and laying his mug on the countertop, turned his back to her as he grasped the Formica edges with his hands and stared out the window. "At one time, I did want...and expect...to be a family man. I married when I was twenty-seven, my bride was a year younger. Susan Black-Mellis. Daughter of the real-estate Black-Mellises of Calgary. You already know she was beautiful—she also had an impeccable background, and was active in local politics. I thought she would make a perfect wife...and a perfect mother." His voice was muffled. "I'd never made any secret of the fact that I wanted a family—my dream was to have a couple of kids, so I could lavish on them the kind of love I had been blessed with as a child. She assured me she wanted a family too...and we began working on it right away."

Capri felt a shaft of jealousy as she listened to his frank words. "You...haven't mentioned love. Were you? In love with her, I mean?"

She saw the knitted fabric of his teal-blue sweater strain over his suddenly tautened shoulders. "I thought so, in the beginning. But...gradually I began to see her in a different light. She didn't seem to be the same woman as the one I married. She changed."

"In what way?"

"My job entails a lot of traveling, and my schedule is unpredictable—during our engagement, she never complained about my frequent absences. But right after our honeymoon she told me she wanted me to take an administrative post in the city, a nine-to-five job which would ensure I could be home every night——"

"But wouldn't that be natural for a new bride?" Capri murmured, trying to see both sides of the story. "If she was in love with you, she would want you with her..."

"She wanted me with her," he ground out, "but not for the reasons you think. She wanted to 'tame' me, as she put it, to mold me into the kind of man who would make her the envy of her friends when I escorted her to all the glitzy Calgary functions which were her life blood..."

What was it Zoe had said when she'd talked about Susan having tried to change Taggart? Capri clearly recalled the contemptuously spoken words. "She might as well have tried to turn the tide—it would have been easier... Taggart Smith is his own man and *that* will never change." Capri could tell from the determined set of Taggart's body that Zoe had been right.

"I was *damned* if I was going to be a lapdog for any woman!" Taggart's ferocious words snapped her attention quickly back to the present. "I refused... adamantly," he went on. "We argued about it...and the arguments got more and more heated—more and more bitter. Finally, after a year and a half, she demanded a divorce. By that time I was only too eager to comply."

"You said once that your divorce was messy." Capri played abstractedly with the handle of her mug. "In what way?"

He swung around, his blue eyes cold and hard. "Susan felt her inability to change me made her lose face with her friends, so she used every dirty trick in the book to discredit me in court. That I could forgive... but what I *couldn't* forgive..."

Capri sat forward in her chair, her gaze glued to him.

"What I couldn't forgive was the treachery I discovered only after the divorce." The words seemed torn from him. "She waited till everything was finalized, then she took a vicious delight in telling me that when she couldn't persuade me to give up my job she had decided to exact punishment by going on the Pill without my knowledge."

He pushed himself violently away from the countertop and resumed his restless pacing. "But she was too late. What she hadn't realized at the time was—she was already pregnant. When she found out about it, she kept her condition a secret from me."

Capri felt an apprehensive chill ripple through her. "What... what happened?"

He looked away from her, as if he couldn't bear for her to see the expression in his eyes. For a long moment he didn't speak. When he did, his voice had a strangled quality. "She went to a clinic and had our baby aborted. It was a boy. He would have been seven this year. Every time I walk along the beach, I picture him playing there."

In the silence that followed, Capri vaguely heard the crackle of the logs in the fire, the wind gusting over the corrugated tin roof of the cabin. She stared at Taggart, at the anguish apparent in every line of his body. She longed to run to him, to comfort him, but she was afraid to try to penetrate the invisible wall of his grief.

She hugged her arms around herself, suddenly chilled despite the warmth in the room. There were no words adequate to express the horror she felt.

He turned to face her and the lost look in his eyes made her want to weep. "Seeing Ellen today—seeing her shine with her own special beauty as she looked at her child—I had to wonder just what kind of a woman I had married...and I had to wonder about my judgment. How could I have been so *blind*? And when I looked at little Samuel, I felt as if my heart was being ripped into tiny pieces..."

"Oh, Taggart..." Capri pushed her chair back and stood up, facing him. Roughly, she wiped away the tears that she could feel welling in her eyes. She couldn't bear it, to see him so unhappy, so tormented. "I wish there was something I could say...or do... I feel so helpless..."

"For God's sake." His tone was ragged. "I didn't mean to make you cry..."

He crossed the space between them in one stride, and Capri felt herself swept up in a grip that took her breath away as his arms went around her. He pressed her head against his chest, and she could feel the strong hammering of his heart through his sweater. With a sob, she slid her arms around his waist, and began caressing him in an effort to comfort him. How could he have stood it, bringing a baby into the world, knowing what had happened to his own...?

She felt her heartbeats stagger as she suddenly realized he was pressing kisses to her temple, his fingers weaving caressingly through the strands of her hair. "It's magic," he murmured disbelievingly. "*You're* magic. When I hold you in my arms all the pain goes away!"

Capri felt her limbs grow weak. Was she really able to help him that much? If so...

"Then I'll hold you for as long as it takes," she whispered. Her voice was muffled against his chest. "I'll hold you forever, if that's what you want."

She felt him stiffen. Then he held her away from him, his blue gaze smoky and unsure. "Do you know what you're saying?"

Capri didn't try to hide the love in her eyes as she met his penetrating gaze. "Yes," she whispered, "I know exactly what I'm saying."

"Oh, Capri..." He groaned, and held her close again. "Am I dreaming? The thought of you has been driving me wild. Your hair..." He stroked it tenderly. "It's like silk. It's beautiful. Your face, your eyes...everything's beautiful. And that incredibly erotic and alluring body..." His words were swollen with longing. "I want you, Jones." He tangled one hand in her hair and cupped the back of her head with his hand, drawing her toward him.

Capri's heart was beating so hard that she thought it might burst. Jones. He was calling her Jones again. Just as he had in the beginning, but now, instead of the teasing she had always heard in it, she could hear only raw desire. She could hear it in his husky tone—and she could feel it in the electrical tension that once again coiled tautly between them. "How can you want me," she asked faintly, "after the things I said that night on the beach? You were so angry with me——"

"No," he said gently, "not angry." He framed her face with his hands, and the intensity of his gaze sent a shudder spiraling through her. "Oh, for a moment I was...I'm not denying that. But my anger didn't last. When I saw you storming away, a moon-silvered goddess as you sped along the beach with your hair flying behind you like shining wings, I knew in a blinding flash why you had said what you did. You were jealous. Jealous of Zoe."

Shame made Capri lower her eyes. "You're right," she whispered. "I was jealous of her. I'm truly sorry, Taggart, for having been so horrid."

"You had no reason to be jealous." He pressed a soft kiss on each dipped eyelid. "There's never been anything between Zoe and me."

"You...you didn't go to her cabin—that night when I slept in your bed?"

"Good Lord, no!" Taggart was obviously appalled. "I took a sleeping bag and spent the night under the stars."

Relief flowed through Capri in a warm, joyous stream. "But you seem so...close."

"Our families have always lived next door to each other. Her father, Tom, is my partner. He's much older than I am, and was widowed shortly after Zoe's birth. Though he hired a housekeeper, Trace brought the baby to our place a lot, and spent every moment she could mothering her, so Zoe's always been like another sister to me. She's studying to be a forester, and she's been taking care of the cabins for three summers now—and doing a good job."

"She seems to believe taking care of you is part of that job!" Capri's lips twisted wryly.

"She's been protective of me ever since Susan and I divorced. I think she sensed that Susan had betrayed me in some way, and didn't want that to happen again. So she took it upon herself to chase away any woman who seemed to...want me. I knew what she was doing...and I must admit," he added ruefully, "at times she came in handy." He kissed Capri's temple. "I even used her to keep you at a distance."

Capri's eyes widened. "You *did*?"

"Mm. That night on the beach, when you stormed away from me, I realized my feelings for you were getting out of hand. That was when I knew just how badly I wanted you...and I must say it shook me. I deliberately cavorted with Zoe outside your cabin next morning to convince you that whatever had been between you and me was over——"

"You *what*?"

"—and I deliberately let you believe I was still angry with you, to put up another barrier between us...when all the time I was longing to sweep you into my arms. Lord, how I wanted you. Still want you. Do *you*, Jones? Want me, I mean?"

The husky, sexy timbre of his voice sent a thrill of excitement and desire through Capri, so strong that it took her breath away. She swallowed, finding her throat painfully dry, and, before she could answer, he murmured, "We were meant to make love, Jones. It was ordained from the moment we met."

Deep in her heart, Capri knew he was right. And the knowledge made her afraid. She had sworn never to let herself become vulnerable again...and now it was too late. She couldn't deny this man anything.

"Yes," she whispered, her fingers clutching his sweater, her mouth raised to his. "I know."

Desire smoked in his dark-pupilled eyes. "You have the most delectable lips in the world...red, full, enticing as a ripe strawberry. But I'm not going to kiss them—at least, not here, because if I start I won't stop, and I don't want to make love to you on the floor. Put your arms around my neck." The order was given softly. "And don't let go."

Bewildered, she raised her hands and wove her fingers together at his nape. "Like this?" she asked weakly.

"Hold tight."

He swung her off her feet, and Capri gasped. "What...? Where are you taking me?"

For a moment she thought he was going to carry her into her bedroom. But instead he strode towards the outside door and opened it. "I'm taking you to my place——" he kicked the door shut behind him, and the sound cracked in the stillness of the morning "—because I've no intention of making love to you with another man's portrait looking down at us."

Capri felt herself tense. She jerked up her head and looked at Taggart. "You don't understand!" She was barely aware of the chill salt-tanged breeze blowing in from the ocean. "It's not what you think. Jamie and I were——"

He interrupted her quickly. "No explanations, not now. We can——"

"But I want you to know what——"

A swift kiss brushed her lips, sealing them. "Later," he murmured determinedly, "later we'll talk. This isn't the time."

Capri held her breath for a moment, words bursting to be spoken, and then exhaled softly. Relax, she told herself, relax. He was right—now wasn't the time for talking. Now was the time for loving. There would be plenty of time for talk, for explanations, afterward.

Afterward... She tightened her grip around his neck as her mind flew forward to what awaited her in Taggart's cabin. Whatever he wanted of her, she was ready to give... She felt as if she'd been waiting all her life for this moment.

As he strode under the trees cutting their path to the log building, the breeze scurried among the branches, and a fine shower of water from the needles and leaves scattered lightly over them.

"Mother Nature's throwing her own brand of confetti over us." Taggart looked down at her without slowing his pace, his blue eyes more serious than she'd ever seen them. "You look like a bride," he said in a voice thick with emotion, "in that white robe, and with all those raindrops sparkling in your hair..."

Capri felt a delicious shiver of anticipation rake through her at his words. She *felt* like a bride. A bride about to be initiated into the wonders of love, the mystery of sex. Her deepest instincts told her that making love with Taggart Smith would be an experience to be treasured, cherished...

The warmth from the kitchen stove enveloped Capri as he locked the door behind them and carried her around the table and into the bedroom. The smell of burning cedar logs drifted to her nostrils, and as she inhaled it she knew that she would for evermore associate the evocative fragrance with this day. With this man.

He pulled back the covers and laid her on his bed as carefully, as tenderly, as if she were a priceless porcelain figurine.

"I'm going to put some logs on the stove, to make sure we stay warm. I'll be right back." His gaze clung to hers for an endless moment, as if he couldn't bring himself to leave. "Don't go away." He brushed the curve of her cheekbone with the back of his hand and let his fingers linger gently.

As he finally walked away across the room, Capri sank back weakly against the pillows, the husky promise in his words echoing in her heart.

She was glad she had just washed her hair—she pulled a strand to her nostrils and breathed in the sweet fragrance of her shampoo. She was glad that her body was warm and her skin silky, glad that after she'd washed she'd dusted herself all over with her favorite talc. Heart hammering, she ran her fingers over the fabric of her robe. When she had slipped it on after washing her hair, she hadn't dreamed this would happen ... She was completely naked under it. A wave of excitement trembled through her...

She heard Taggart pumping the water and realized he had finished with the stove, and was washing the woodsmoke from his hands. He'd be coming back any minute.

Snuggling her face into the pillow, she closed her eyes. If she pretended to be asleep, she would be able to avoid watching him take off his clothes. With an effort, she managed to steady her breathing so that it sounded regular...

She heard his step come through the doorway, and then heard him pause. For a moment there was no sound in the room except her breathing.

Then she heard him swear.

"Damn!" His voice was barely audible, but there was no mistaking his frustration. "She's fallen asleep. I guess she's tired out, after having been up all night. I could go for a hike around the island, I suppose... Maybe by the time I get back she'll be awake."

Capri stiffened. *What?* He was going to leave her? He couldn't... not after he'd built her up to expect...

Before she could move, she heard the shuffle of his feet, heard the bedroom door click shut. Oh, no...

She pushed the covers back and sat up. "Taggart!" she called out. "Wait! Come b——"

She stopped short with a gasp as she saw his tall blond figure leaning indolently against the wall, just inside the door. He'd been there all the time! His grin was cocky, teasing... the same grin she'd seen on his face that very first afternoon when she'd come storming into his cabin looking for the caretaker...

"You *beast*!" She tried to sound stern but the bubble of laughter rising up inside her couldn't be restrained. "I thought you'd gone," she spluttered.

"Gone?" There was no mistaking the gentle menace in his tone as he advanced toward her, tugging his sweater up from his waist.

Capri's gaze flickered to his bare chest. In a moment she would be able to run her fingers through the enticing swirl of hair, she thought with a pulse of excitement— able to caress his smoothly gleaming shoulders, able to lay a hand over his heart and feel its steady drum-beat——

"No way," he went on. "I was up all night too. I need to catch up on my beauty sleep." He bent down and took off his running shoes.

He wasn't wearing socks—did he ever wear any? Capri wondered absently.

He looked up and it was as if he had read the question in her eyes. "I don't even own a pair, Jones. They would restrict my freedom—you see, I like to wiggle my toes..."

He chuckled, but the desire in his eyes sent darts of answering desire quivering through Capri with almost painful intensity. She slid to the opposite side of the bed from where he was standing, and, curling up into a ball, laid her head on the pillow. Clasping her hands under her cheek, she peeked up at him through the silky strands of her hair. "Sleep?" She tried to keep her voice steady. "Is that what you plan to do?"

"Unless you can come up with some other way to pass the time on such a cold, dreary day." He unbuckled the heavy silver belt buckle at his waist, and his gaze glinted challengingly as he reached for the zip of his jeans.

Capri squeezed her eyelids shut. She kept them shut as she heard the rasp of the zip being opened, kept them shut as she heard the rustle of jeans being pulled off, kept them shut as she felt the mattress dip under his weight.

She thought she heard a chuckle, but he made no attempt to slide over beside her, no attempt to touch her. Tentatively she opened her eyes, and her heart gave a gigantic leap as she looked into a sapphire gaze that was bright with amusement. His head was on the other pillow, and he was so near that she could feel his warm breath on her cheek. It held the lingering fragrance of coffee.

"Do you always sleep curled up like a dormouse?" Laughter lilted in his voice, enhancing the undertone of desire. "I'm disappointed, Jones. I must admit I've thought about you often—of how you'd look in your bed—and I always pictured you lying on your back, with erotic abandon, your hair fanning out over the pillow, your breasts tantalizingly thrusting up under the covers.''

"Life's full of disappointments, isn't it?'' Capri was delighted with her light lazy drawl. "And I'm surprised you haven't had anything better to do than spend your time picturing how I look when I'm in my bed asleep!''

"Ah, but I have!'' he mocked. "I've spent much more time picturing how you would look in *my* bed when you're *not* asleep—ouch! You didn't have to kick me——''

Capri choked back a nervous giggle as he burrowed under the covers and all she could see was his bare back as he caught hold of the offending foot. A bare back that was so beautiful that she wanted to run her palms over it . . .

"Socks!'' His muffled tone was outraged. "You wear socks in bed! Ah, how sadly disillusioned I am to learn that you are guilty of such a spinsterish habit . . .''

He surfaced again with a suddenness that caught Capri by surprise, and captured her in his arms. She felt every cell, every nerve in her body spring to excruciating awareness of him as her soft feminine curves were drawn tightly against his hard, muscular frame.

"But I *am* a spinster,'' she protested breathlessly. "You must know that a spinster is an unmarried woman!''

"She's also a woman who spins,'' he growled, contorting his handsome features into an accusing scowl, "and you've been spinning a web around me from the moment you came into my life . . .'' He buried his face in the delicate scented hollow at the base of her throat. "A web,'' he went on in a low murmur, "from which I have no desire to escape.''

As he brushed her smooth sensitive skin with his lips, Capri felt a quiver ripple through her. If she had spun a web around him, it had been done without her conscious will. But he in turn, with his rugged good looks, his beguiling charm, and his deep sensitivity, had spun a web of his own—one in which her heart and soul were hopelessly entangled.

And one which had seduced her into a situation for which she was in no way prepared. As the implications of what was about to happen between them fully dawned on her, she drew back, a flush of color on her cheekbones.

"Taggart..." She hesitated.

"What is it?" He framed her face with his hands and forced her to meet his eyes. "Have I said something to upset you? Why are you...blushing?" He caressed her cheeks lightly with his thumbs, his tone wondering.

Capri dipped her eyelashes in attempt to veil the embarrassment in her expression. "It's just that...I...I'm not on the——"

"Ah." He drew a fingertip over her parted lips. "You don't have to worry about that. I'd never do anything to hurt you, Capri..."

His tenderness, his concern, caused an exquisite pain to cut through her. She turned her face and pressed a kiss against his palm. "I know you wouldn't," she whispered.

"No more problems?"

"No more problems..."

"Good..." With a sweep of his arm, he pushed the bedcovers down to their waists and gave a sigh of satisfaction as he freed them of the encumbrance.

Capri felt the breath catch in her throat as he ran his fingers down the lapels of her robe to the four round pearl buttons which fastened it. He swiftly tugged them open, his warm fingers leaving a trail of fire on her skin everywhere they touched, a fire that burned like a brand, making her his. At last he slipped his hands under the heavy silk fabric, pushing it away from her breasts and exposing them.

"Dear heaven..." She heard the aching disbelief in his voice, his reaction to her nakedness so intense that she found herself closing her eyes. Tautly, she threw her head sideways on her pillow and as she did she heard a low, almost inaudible moan. And then there was silence, except for his quickened breathing, and she knew he was looking at her body...

A shudder raked through her as she felt him cup the swollen flesh of her breasts, felt him support them in his hands, testing their weight, familiarizing himself with their shape. She was glad they were firm and full, glad they were nicely shaped, high and round... her limbs felt heavy as he slowly, lovingly, brushed the tender tips with lips that were seeking and moist, and desire swept over her in great, drowning waves, like the surge of the ocean over the shore at high tide, as he began suckling them in turn, tugging with his teeth, licking with his tongue. Playing with them. Worshiping them. Driving her to distraction!

She was conscious of nothing but his touch—his mouth on her breasts, his hands going around her as he slid her arms out of the robe and tossed it over his shoulder. She opened her eyes in time to see it flutter to the floor, like a white parachute.

"Not fair," she whispered, astonished at the thick huskiness of her tone, "I'm naked now, and you're not."

"You want to be fair?" His palms skimmed fleetingly, teasingly, over her nipples and she felt a fierce influx of blood to the soft buds. They tightened abruptly, greedy for a more lingering touch. She hadn't realized they were so incredibly sensitive; hadn't realized that such feather-light caresses could make her feel as ecstatic and dizzy as if she were whirling on an out-of-control merry-go-round! "Then you must undress me," Taggart's lips curved in a lopsided smile, "just as I undressed you!"

She hadn't looked at him as he slid into bed beside her, but when he'd pulled her close, she'd become aware he was still wearing his jockey shorts. He wanted her to take them off? Capri swallowed, and licked suddenly dry lips. "No, I can't..."

"Shy, Jones?" His voice held the same challenge as his eyes had held when he had reached for the zip of his jeans.

This time she wasn't going to shrink from it. "As a matter of fact I am, Mr. Smith——"

"Well, in that case, I'm afraid——"

"—but I won't let that stop me."

When he had pushed back the covers earlier, the top sheet had somehow twined itself around his thighs. Holding her breath, Capri tugged it free, and, grasping the elastic waistband of his briefs, said in the brisk, businesslike tone of a nursing orderly, "You'll have to raise your hips, please, so I can slide them off."

She didn't look at his face as he obliged. She didn't look at anything. Her eyes were once again screwed tightly shut. But she could feel the rough hairiness of his thighs as her fingers brushed against them, and the hard bones of his knees, the muscled strength of his calves. His feet were long and bony, and as she slid the briefs over them she noticed they were warm.

She felt flushed and breathless as she raised her head and, following his earlier example, tossed the underwear over her shoulder on to the floor. Painfully conscious of her nakedness, she bent a hand to reach for the sheet to cover herself, but found her fingers caught in Taggart's relentless grip.

"Leave it, Jones." His voice was rough with emotion. "I want to look at you...*and I want you to look at me.*" They were lying on their sides, facing each other, and Capri felt a deep flush rise to cover her cheeks as she heard what he was saying. He wanted her to look at him...but, no matter how she tried, she *knew* she wouldn't be able to bring herself to lower her gaze...

Her eyelids flickered in mute protest as he lifted her hand and placed it on his chest, but as she felt the wiry texture of the short springy curls against her skin a spasm of excitement shot through her. Involuntarily, she glanced down, and her racing pulse quickened further as she noticed the contrast between her slender, fine-boned fingers and the wide, muscled expanse of his chest. Male...female... So different, so tantalizingly, wonderfully different...

Feeling as if she were hypnotized, she let her finger-tips slide through the rough hair, glorying in the very masculinity of it. His skin was warm, and it smelled of woodsmoke and soap. Driven by the passion glowing to ardent life inside her, Capri dared to explore beyond the crisp gold curls. And she felt her own breasts swell, the peaks jut in response as, utterly intoxicated by the erotic silkiness under her fingertips, she traced a bold path over one flat brown nipple.

She heard his quick hiss as she teased it lightly, heard him groan as she leaned over and daringly flicked the swiftly hardening bead with the tip of her tongue. As it became taut under her erotic touch, she felt her own breasts ache, felt desire rake through her, settling pain-fully deep in her womb. Compelled by something beyond her control, and elated in her discovery of her power over him, she circled the little bud with her soft, warm lips, and sucked gently.

"So...not so shy after all." Taggart's voice was ragged. "But a brazen temptress..."

Her long hair had fallen over his chest as she had leaned over. Now he swept it back with his hands, and wove his fingers through it, cupping her head and bringing her face so close to his that she could feel the heat of his skin. He dragged her up against him, crushing her breasts against his chest, and capturing her mouth with his own in a kiss that seemed to draw her soul from her. Feverishly, desperately, he moved his lips over hers, demanding a response that Capri was powerless to deny. And when, a slave of her own desire, she found her lower body imprisoned against his thighs, her soft womanhood arrogantly challenged by his unfettered, steel-hard arousal, nothing in the world existed except the sensations flooding her.

Warm flesh, musky scents, irresistible caresses.

Strong, seeking hands slid down to her thighs, cupping the taut curves. His body strained urgently against hers, as if he would mold them together permanently.

And, when finally he twisted her around to lie on her back, she felt the heat that had surged through her at his every touch now flow into only one spot, one burning core of desire, right at her center. She writhed impatiently as she waited for him.

"Steady, my love... Just wait. I told you I'd never do anything to hurt you..."

She watched, her eyes glazed, her lids heavy as he readied himself. Love and lust and desire were all one— now she could look at him and not feel embarrassment—all her inhibitions had gone and she felt as if her body were turning to molten gold...

With a moan, she reached out a trembling hand to help him, and as she ran wondering, worshiping fingertips over the swollen tautness of him she saw him freeze.

"Dear heaven, Capri, don't do that..." His voice was a dark, erotic groan. It sent a shaft of electricity slicing through her, and she sank back helplessly, utterly dazed by the intensity of her feelings for him.

"I'm sorry," she managed, huskily. "It's just that... you're so beautiful...so perfect... I had to touch you..."

There was no sound in the room as their eyes met and locked. She thought she saw a gleam of tears in his, but if they *were* tears she knew they were tears of joy. And joy danced inside her too.

But as he moved over her, and buried his face in her hair, murmuring words that fanned the flames burning inside her, the tears were forgotten.

And all that was left was the sweet, wild, wonderful ecstasy of their desire.

CHAPTER TEN

"WHO was he?" Taggart, straddling one of the kitchen chairs which he'd pulled over to the wood stove, looked away from the wholewheat muffin he was toasting at the open fire, and directed a steady glance at Capri.

She was lazily curled up in an old rocking chair right beside him, dreamily staring into the bright flames. How feminine and fragile she felt, she mused, with nothing on but this baggy gray sweatshirt of Taggart's that came almost to her knees.

He had slipped it over her head when she'd finally awakened from the deep sleep she'd fallen into after they'd made love for a second time, and she had reveled in its enveloping warmth, just as she had reveled in the enveloping warmth of its owner as he'd taken her in his arms once again and held her against his heart——

"I want to know." His voice was quiet, but it interrupted her straying thoughts. "I want to know everything about you. I *need* to know...about him."

Capri blinked, and, reaching over, ran a tenderly caressing hand up his forearm. "I'm sorry." A rueful smile curved her mouth. "I was dreaming..."

"About me, I hope?" he said levelly.

She shook her head. "About *us*. I was thinking how safe and secure I feel with you..."

The tantalizing smell of cinnamon and raisins drifted into the air as the muffin browned. Taggart turned it on the fork and said, with a tightening of his lips, "If it's not too painful still, tell me about him—tell me about the bastard who hurt you so much."

157

"Oh, Taggart—he was no... bastard. He was sweet, and charming, and everyone loved him. He would never knowingly have hurt anyone..." She bit her lip as she saw Taggart's eyes cloud over. Was he jealous? Remorse flooded her, and she hurried on, "Remember I told you about my mother? Jamie was so like her—they were both risk-takers, always looking for thrills, courting danger——"

"Capri——" There was a note of grim warning in his voice.

"He wasn't a lover, Taggart," she rushed to reassure him. "He was my brother. My twin brother, Jamie. I adored him. I just couldn't have imagined life without him. But he died a week after we both turned twenty-one."

There was a long silence between them as Taggart stared at her, obviously sorting out all the facts of which he was now in possession, and discarding all the mistaken conclusions he'd come to. Then he shook his head wearily. "Oh, God, Capri, I'm sorry. What more can I say?" He made a helpless gesture. "My own sister is very much alive...and, though she's older than I am, and has her own life now with her husband and son, I can't begin to imagine life without her. But to have lost a twin... Damn, why didn't I guess...when you talked of your 'other half'?" A frown creased his brow. "But the photograph by your bed...I didn't see any resemblance."

"We weren't alike in any way." Capri slid the toasted muffin from the end of the fork as he abstractedly held it out to her. "We didn't look alike, we didn't act alike. He took after my mother's side of the family, and I took after my father's. We were absolute opposites...just as Maddy and Jake were opposites——"

"Jake? Your father?" Taggart absently tapped the toasting fork against the chair.

"Mm. Jake and I are both too serious, too intense—too cautious. We don't like taking risks——"

"You took a bit of a risk coming here." Taggart leaned over and, framing Capri's face between his hands, captured her mouth in a kiss that took her breath away. He sat back again, his eyes lingering on the bruised fullness of her lips. "Coming to a place you knew nothing about."

"It was a small risk—but, even so, it's had its price!"

"Its price?"

Capri grimaced. "My father has been trying to marry me off for the past several years. He's absolutely desperate to have a grandchild. In the past, he's always arranged my holidays for me, and I haven't minded—except that he has always tried to set me up, so I've spent my vacations ducking away from ardent suitors. This year, however, I outfoxed him!" With a chuckle, Capri outlined the trick she had played on her father, the trick that, admittedly, had backfired. "The last thing I expected to find on Blueberry Island was a man like you. I still can't believe this has happened."

"This?"

Capri blushed. "That I've let myself become involved. I came here to work—and now I find myself caught up in a summer affair..."

"A summer affair? Is that what you call it?"

"Well, yes, I would." Capri looked puzzled. "Wouldn't you?"

"I'd prefer to think of it as a...courtship."

Blue velvet. Again she was being caressed by eyes that were luring her with seductive invitation. The creaking of her rocking-chair gradually slowed to a halt. "A... courtship?"

"Do you think your father will approve of me?"

Capri stiffened, and blinked. What did he mean? Approve of him for...what?

"As a potential father for his future grandchildren."

As Taggart spoke, Capri wondered dizzily if she'd asked her question aloud. But she knew she hadn't. She stared at Taggart, feeling the blood drain from her cheeks. She had fallen in love with him, but she hadn't let herself think any further than this moment. He had never said anything about love...yet...he was asking her to marry him?

"I...don't understand," she said in a faint voice. "Surely you're not...asking what I think you're asking?"

His eyes were so serious that she felt the skin at her nape prickle. "I'm asking you to marry me, Capri."

He got up abruptly and pushed his chair aside. While she was still trying to collect her scattered senses, he removed the toasted muffin from her suddenly nerveless fingers and tossed it on to the table along with the fork. Then, pulling her to her feet, he put his arms around her and drew her close. "I know it's happened quickly, but that's the way it does sometimes. And, even if I waited ten years, I know I couldn't be more sure than I am at this moment that we were made for each other." His lips brushed her brow tenderly. "I love you, my sweet Jones, and I want you to be my wife. I want to love you forever, I want us to have children together. You stole my heart away that very first day when you came charging into my cabin..."

Capri was glad he was holding her so tightly. She felt her knees buckle, and she slid her arms quickly around his neck and clung to him, her eyes swimming with emotion. "Oh, Taggart," she said with a catch in her voice, "can this be really happening? It's like a dream."

"Just tell me it's a dream that you want to make true."

"Oh, I do. I love you too, more than I ever thought possible——"

She started, and broke off abruptly as a harsh staccato sound interrupted her emotional words, and shattered the drowsy calm of the cabin. "What's that?" she gasped, drawing her arms from his neck and grasping his hands. "Is there someone outside?"

Taggart closed his eyes, his expression tight. "Oh, damn it to hell!" he muttered. "Not now, for heaven's sake!"

"What is it?" Capri couldn't keep the anxiety from her voice. "What's wrong?"

"Nothing," he said wryly, "and everything. It's my radio... my office, calling from Calgary." He buried his face in her hair, inhaling the sweet fragrance of her shampoo. "I'll be back in a minute..."

He raised her hands to his lips and, brushing a kiss over the fingertips, he released her and strode quickly across the kitchen and into the living room.

Capri's legs felt like jelly, and she sank back gratefully into the cushioned rocking chair. She closed her eyes, and leaning back against the slats, started the chair rocking.

He loved her... she loved him. She had never expected this to happen, but now that it had she felt as if she was floating on top of the world, on a fluffy white cloud, with sunshine all around. She had never in her life felt so safe, so protected. She would marry Taggart, and they would live happily ever after.

Jake would be delighted. Taggart, she knew, was his kind of man. A man you could count on. A man you could trust. How foolish she had been to fight her attraction to him. There had been no danger after all, but a haven!

She cocked her ear toward the living room, but, though she could hear the murmur of Taggart's voice, his words were unintelligible. Ellen had said he was a "mystery man". Capri found herself chuckling. When he came back into the kitchen, she would find out what he did for a living—and, she realized wryly, she would have to explain who she was too. She hoped he didn't have any objections to marrying an heiress——

"Dear heavens, but you look beautiful." Taggart's voice broke into her thoughts. "Did I ever tell you your hair looks like chocolate silk?"

Capri opened her eyes to see him leaning against the doorjamb, his expression vulnerable with love.

She curved her lips in a seductive smile. "Did I ever tell you that the first time I saw you I guessed you wanted to whisk me into bed with you?"

"You did?" He pushed himself from the doorway and walked toward her with his arms open. "And how did you feel about that?"

She got to her feet and walked into his embrace. "Confused! I admitted to myself that you were incredibly sexy, the most gorgeous specimen of manhood I'd ever seen, but..." She hesitated. Now would be the perfect time to tell him who she was. "Remember when I pretended to be a writer?"

"Mm." He nibbled her lobe, and she squirmed with pleasure. "I certainly do. Tell me...what on earth induced you to make up that particular story?"

"I was upset because I found myself so strongly drawn—physically—to someone with whom I had apparently nothing in common. And as I looked at you, I suddenly had this vision of a headline in one of those confession magazines—and that's what sparked the idea."

He played with a strand of her hair, running his lips along it, his expression teasing as he said, "What kind of a headline was it? A 'Beauty falls in love with the Beast' kind of thing?"

"More of a 'Texan oil heiress attracted to a penniless caretaker' kind of thing," she said quietly. Biting her lip, she found herself holding her breath as she waited for his reaction.

He frowned and looked at her blankly. "An *oil* heiress? You're not an..."

Capri grimaced ruefully.

"You *are* an...?"

At Capri's nodded response, his brows shot up, his expression as amazed as if he'd been shot in the back by an arrow. "Good Lord." He shook his head. "Capri Jones." He rolled the name gently on his tongue... and then as she watched, she saw a look of stunned comprehension gradually dawn in his eyes. "Well, I'll be damned!" he said slowly. "Jones Oil? Your father's *that* Jake Jones?"

"You know him?" Capri leaned back a little and stared up at him. "You *know* my father?"

"We've met," he drawled nonchalantly, "a couple of times."

"But how? Where? I've never heard him mention your name."

He pulled her closer. "You don't know who I am, do you?" It was a flat statement, not a question.

"Of course I don't—you know I don't!" Capri said impatiently. "Ellen told me you keep your private life very private, and that no one on the island knows what you do for a living." She reached up and teasingly tugged a strand of blond hair that had fallen over his brow. "Don't you think it's time to let me in on your deep dark secret?"

"Ellen was right—I do try to keep a low profile when I'm on the island. I don't get here as often as I'd like, but when I do come, I want to enjoy total privacy. Nobody knows me—except, of course, Zoe!—and I can relax——"

"I'm not a patient woman, Mr. Smith," Capri said warningly.

"Okay, okay." He grinned. "I'll get to the point. You've heard of Smith and Garson, the oil well fire-fighting and blow-out specialists?"

"Well, of course... Even if I didn't work in the oil industry, I expect I would have—they're world famous. As a matter of fact, Garson recently controlled an offshore blow-out and fire for Jake in Venezuela. Smith and——" Capri stopped, hearing her own words echoing in the air, over and over again. She shivered. Her blood had stopped running—it must have; she felt as if it had suddenly turned to ice. Her whole body felt as if it was numb. "Smith and Garson?" she whispered. "*Smith* and Garson? You're *that* Smith?" Her voice trembled fearfully. "Oh, please God, no, say you're not that Smith——"

"Capri, what in the name of heaven is the——?"

"No, no, no!" she cried. "Tell me it's not true." She clenched her hands into fists and pummeled them against his chest. "You're lying, you're lying..."

"Take it easy, now, take it easy." Taggart gripped her wrists and, holding them tightly, pulled them hard against his chest so that she couldn't move. "What did I say?" She could hear the pleading, the bewilderment in his tone. "For Pete's sake, Capri, tell me what's wrong!"

She struggled to keep back the sobs that were building up inside her. She had to be calm—screaming and crying would achieve nothing. What a fool she'd been! She had let herself fall in love, had let herself be lulled into believing that she had miraculously met a man with whom she would be safe, a man who would make sure she was never hurt again. And already she could feel his hands on her heart, twisting it, tearing it, ripping it in two...

Swallowing the huge lump that had formed in her throat, she tried to keep her voice even. "You can let me go now, Taggart. I'm sorry, I shouldn't have done that... lost control..." As his grip slackened slightly, she snatched her hands away. Then, slipping quickly from him before he could catch her, she went to stand by the sink, with her back to the window. She didn't want the light to be shining on her face, revealing every little nuance of her anguish.

"You chose an extremely dangerous profession." She slid her hands behind her back and twined her fingers together fiercely to stop them shaking.

"Yes," he said, carefully. "It can be dangerous."

She clamped her teeth together to stop them from chattering, and spoke through them. "Fire...is a terrifying thing. Unpredictable. Consuming. You must often take great risks..."

"The risks are there...but every day new techniques are being developed to make the job safer——"

"Risks." Capri looked at him but saw only a blur. "Jamie took risks. He sought out danger. Did I tell you he was a racing-car driver?"

Vaguely she heard his taut, "No, you didn't, Capri."

Dully, she went on. "Strange, how alike he and Maddy were. Not only in the way they lived, but in the way they died. Maddy crashed her small plane, and it exploded in an inferno. Jamie crashed his car while racing in Europe... He might have come out of it alive, but he was trapped in the wreckage, and it went on fire before he could be rescued... Jake and I were watching it on television. They told us later that his body was burned beyond recognition—that it would be better if we didn't see it."

The silence that vibrated between them was so intense that Capri felt herself hunching over as if in pain. From a distance, she heard Taggart's anguished, "Capri, I'm not like your mother, or Jamie—I don't court danger, I don't seek risks——"

Capri closed her eyes. "Perhaps you don't, Taggart. But whether or not you court danger, or seek risks, the danger and the risks are still there." She turned from him, and raising her heavy eyelids, stared unseeingly out the window. "That call you got a few minutes ago...you have to go? A blow-out? A fire?"

She could feel the power of his emotion pulling at her, drawing her to face him. She resisted, gripping the edge of the countertop to keep herself from doing something she would regret.

"Yes. In Alberta. Brock is coming to pick me up in an hour." She'd never heard his voice so harsh before. "Capri, for pity's sake, will you *listen* to me? I know you've gone through a lot...but you can't hide from life...you can't run away from it. Sure I face risks...but, whether you like it or not, so do you! You face them every morning when you get up, damn it! You could trip and fall downstairs, you could get hit by a bus when you're crossing the street——"

"No!" Capri whirled around, feeling as if she was sinking, choking, in a quicksand. "It's not the same, Taggart. If I'm careful, I won't fall downstairs. If I'm careful, I won't get hit by a bus. And I *am* careful. *Very* careful. Far too careful to marry someone whose job necessitates him literally walking into raging fires!"

Taggart's face was drawn and haggard, sweat ran down his brow. "Capri, I need you." The words were drawn agonisingly from his lips. "Don't do this to me...to us. *Please,* my sweet love. Not after we've found each other..."

Capri knew that if she didn't leave now she was going to break down. And if she broke down, he would take her in his arms, and, once cradled in his embrace, she knew that her flimsy defenses would collapse like so much rubble. She couldn't let that happen. She had barely managed to hang on to life after she lost Jamie...to be married to a man who faced danger every time he left her would gradually destroy her. "I'm sorry..."

"Capri..."

The pain in his voice stabbed her heart and she felt her body tremble violently. She didn't look at him as she ran to the door. She knew there would be tears in his eyes, and she knew that if she saw them her heart would betray her.

Hardly aware of the cold air against her skin or the wet earth beneath her bare feet, she raced along the path toward the trees. And as she came out on the other side, she heard, carried to shore on the gusting wind, the steady sound of an outboard motor. Breath rasping in her throat, she threw a fleeting glance towards the ocean, and saw the *Blueberry Blazer* about half a mile from the jetty.

The caretaker, returning to the island...

Would Zoe spot her? And would she wonder why she was running wildly through the long wet grass from Taggart's cabin wearing only an oversized sweatshirt? Capri realized she didn't care. All she cared about was putting as much space between herself and Taggart as possible, and as quickly as possible.

Once inside her own cabin, she locked the door behind her, and, running across the kitchen to her bedroom, flung herself on top of the bed and gave in to the pain that was tearing remorselessly at her heart.

Drowned in her despair, and exhausted by all that had happened, she must have drifted off to sleep.

The deafening roar of a helicopter engine woke her. She lay for a moment, disorientated, and then, tiredly dragging her tear-damp hair from her face, she pushed herself off the bed and stumbled through to the kitchen. Her heart seemed to lodge in her throat as she looked out of the window and saw Taggart stride from beyond the trees. He was wearing a rugged brown leather jacket, tight-fitting jeans that revealed the muscled strength of his long legs, and leather cowboy boots... and even though there was twenty yards between them she could feel the powerful magnetism that surrounded him like an aura.

He crouched low as he approached the helicopter at a run, and Capri saw his blond hair go flying around his head, swept by the fierce wind from the rotor blades just above him. Brock was standing in the doorway, a welcoming grin on his face.

Capri clasped her arms round her shivering body as Taggart paused on the step. He seemed to move in slow motion when he turned and looked directly toward the window. Her heartbeats thudded heavily. Could he see her? Had he known she'd be standing there? Was he hoping she would change her mind?

He would never guess how she wanted to, she thought in anguish as she drank in this last sight of him—this last sight of the man she'd come to love. He would never guess how she longed to run after him, tell him she hadn't meant what she said, tell him she'd wait for him. Forever, if necessary . . .

The pilot touched his arm, and said something. Capri saw him nod, and then he turned away abruptly and went into the cabin. The sliding door was pulled into place, and, a moment later, the skids lifted gently from the firm sand, and the helicopter buzzed upward into the sky like a giant metal insect.

Capri watched—through eyes that were blurred with tears, and with a heart that was breaking—till all she could see was a tiny dot on the horizon.

Then, turning from the window, and wiping her damp cheeks with the back of her sleeve, she walked slowly through to her bedroom and sat slumped over, on the edge of the bed, her head in her hands.

It was time to go home.

CHAPTER ELEVEN

"YOUR usual?" Jake lifted a bottle of white wine from a cooler and threw his daughter a questioning glance.

He took a sip of his drink and began fumbling in the pocket of his shirt for a cigar. "Well, Cap," he said, "how was your holiday? Where did you decide to go? Scotland, Spain, or California?"

She took a deep breath. "I went to Blueberry Island."

There was a long pause while Jake went through the ritual of lighting his cigar. Compressing her lips, Capri let her glance move to the portrait that hung above the mantelpiece, a portrait of her mother in a silvery-blue evening gown. Her ash-blond hair was swept up elegantly, her aristocratic features were perfectly composed, and her slender hands were folded calmly in her lap, but the portraitist had cleverly captured the impatience in her clear blue eyes...impatience at having to sit still, when there was a wonderful world outside, just waiting to be conquered...

"How was it, Cappy? Blueberry Island?"

"How was it?" Though she tried to speak steadily, Capri could hear the tremor in her voice. "Oh, I'll tell you exactly how it was! I was terrified out of my wits by a bear one night when I was coming back from the outhouse; I helped deliver a baby in the middle of a storm that almost swept the island off the face of the earth; and——" she paused and took a deep breath, glad of the Dutch courage instilled by the wine "—I fell in love with a man who makes a living by walking into fire!"

Jake Jones wouldn't have been the successful businessman he was, Capri acknowledged bitterly, had

169

he not been able to swiftly sift through a mass of information and extract the relevant facts, leaving the rest to be mulled over later. "Fell in love, eh?" His gray-green eyes were thoughtful, and he chewed on the end of his cigar. "Tell me—did *he* fall in love with *you*?"

Once again, Jake had cut straight to the heart of the matter. Capri felt her cheeks grow warm. She pressed her fingertips against them, noting absently how cold her hands were. "Yes," she said, so quietly her words were almost inaudible, "he did...I believe...fall in love with me."

That morning she'd cut a dozen perfect yellow roses from the garden, and, after arranging them in a silver goblet, had set them on a table in the library. She suddenly became very aware of their rich scent as it mingled with the aroma of Jake's cigar. She glanced at the perfect blossoms in their sophisticated container...and all at once her mind's eye substituted the masses of floppy blue wildflowers Jake had gathered for her, the flowers that had spilled in profusion from the glass vase. The bittersweet memory was like a stab wound in her heart...

"You're crying." Dismay edged her father's voice. He dropped his cigar in an ashtray, and got up. "Cappy," his confusion was obvious, "I've never seen you cry, not since you were a little girl..."

He was right, of course. When her mother had died, she had kept her grief to herself, locked it up inside. When Jamie had died, she had felt as if she had died too. No tears had come. But now, as she looked into her father's bewildered eyes, she felt all her defences collapse, felt as if the floodgates were about to burst.

"I don't understand." He sounded uncharacteristically hesitant. "If you love the man, and he loves you—what's the problem?" He took a few steps toward her.

"You *don't* understand, do you? The reason I've never wanted to marry...it's all tied up with what happened in the past. With the way Maddy and Jamie died." She could no longer control the sobs that had been building up in her chest. "I'm sorry...I know I've never talked about it... About their deaths. Not with you, or anybody else. I know you must have wanted to, but I couldn't." She shook her head helplessly and whispered, "It hurt too much..."

"Oh, dear God." Her father's eyes glistened with sudden tears. "I know how it hurt, sweetheart, and I longed to take you in my arms and comfort you, but you closed me out. You were so tense, so forbidding, so——"

With an aching cry, Capri ran to him, and, putting her arms round him, buried her face against his chest. "I know, I know. I was selfish...I kept my grief locked inside me...and didn't once think how I could have comforted you..."

"How we could have comforted each other." Jake's arms tightened around her till she thought she couldn't breathe. "But it's not too late. We can talk now. We can comfort each other now."

Capri lifted tear-filled eyes. "Oh, Jake, I wanted to die when Jamie did——"

She winced as his grip clenched around her. "Don't say it," he breathed.

"And that's how I feel now. I told Taggart I couldn't see him again." She brushed the back of one hand across her tear-stained cheek. "I hurt him..."

"Hush, hush." He smoothed his palm over her hair. "You can make it up——"

"But I can't!" Capri's voice was despairing. "Don't you see? I can't risk it, Jake. *That's* why I'll never marry. I can't risk loving...and losing...ever again..."

For the next few minutes her sobs echoed in the stillness of the library, punctuated only by Jake's awkwardly murmured "There, there..." as he led her to one of the couches, where she sank down with her face hidden in her hands. When eventually her sobbing quietened, she took a tissue from her pocket, and, blowing her nose fiercely, looked up. Jake was standing with his back to the fireplace, his gaze fixed on her steadily.

"When your mother died," he said in a quiet voice, "I was *furious* with her. I blamed her for the anguish I was experiencing. Why, I asked myself over and over, did she have to be so damned headstrong and *adventurous*? Why couldn't she have been content to do what her contemporaries did—spend her leisure hours playing bridge, attending fashion shows, sitting for hours in beauty salons? Not till I could answer that question honestly did I begin to accept her death."

"How did you answer it?" Capri's voice was wobbly. There could be no answer, she thought despairingly.

"Your mother didn't spend her time doing what the others were doing because she was *Maddy Jones*. And I had to remind myself that that was why I had fallen in love with her in the first place! She was a woman who raced headlong into danger with a courage that took my breath away. If she had been a different person—one who was happy to while away the day in more mundane ways——" Jake shook his head, a reminiscent smile twisting his lips "—she wouldn't have captured my heart the way she did. She was all the things I wasn't, Capri. And that's why I found her so irresistibly fascinating. Only when I realized that, and that I'd rather have had our years together than never have had her at all, was I able to accept her death."

The room was so quiet that Capri could hear the muted ticking of the anniversary clock on the mantel. "And Jamie?" she said huskily. "The same?"

Her heart twisted as she saw the haggard cast his face took on as she mentioned her brother's name. "The same," he said in a low voice. "Though there's no pain like the pain of losing a child..."

For a moment Capri couldn't speak for the tears clogging her throat. And, in that moment, she knew that given a choice between never having known her mother and Jamie, or having shared the years they did have together, she'd still have opted for the latter, despite the anguish she'd suffered when they had died.

Why had she waited so long to share her grief, her feelings, with her father? She wished she could have had the benefit of his wisdom earlier...

"It's a risk, isn't it?" she finally whispered. "A risk you take when you let yourself fall in love."

Jake nodded. "A risk of the heart." He looked at Capri with eyes that shone with love and compassion. "And only you can decide if you're brave enough to take it."

Capri screwed up her nose as she alighted from the cab. Even inside the vehicle, she had smelled the pungent odor of the sour gas from the oil well. Out in the open, despite the strong winds blowing down from the Rockies, it was so strong that she thought it was going to knock her over. And the noise! A thousand jets seemed to be taking off inside her head...

She winced from it, and cupped a hand around her mouth as she shouted to the driver, "I may be some time."

The man glanced happily at his ticking meter, and as Capri turned away he gave her the thumbs-up sign.

She had left her hotel around one-thirty...it had taken almost two hours to drive from Calgary to the Blue Spruce site. The driver had known exactly where to go— the well had been burning out of control for almost two weeks now and everyone in the province, he assured her, was aware of it. In the early hours of that morning, the fire had finally been extinguished.

Her heart was strumming like an overwound clock. She hadn't let Taggart know she was flying up to Calgary.

Would he be annoyed with her for turning up at the site? Should she have waited at her hotel and tried to contact him via his office? And most important of all...would he still want her? Perhaps, now that he'd had time to think things over, he'd decided their island interlude had been, after all, just a summer affair.

Capri pulled her blue suede jacket around her and shivered. It was too late now for dithering. She was here.

And her cream leather boots were going to be ruined, she realized ruefully. The cab driver had parked his vehicle at the end of a gravel road, a good quarter of a mile from the site, and as she walked along this wide track through the forest she sank ankle-deep into mud.

On both sides of her were large trucks, loaded with pipe and equipment, their motors idling. She passed them, her tension rising with every step, and was finally stopped by a barricade, and a gas warning sign.

Danger—Hydrogen Sulphide
Authorized Admission Only

Pressing her hands against her ears in a vain attempt to muffle the almost unbearable noise as the gas screamed from the wellhead, she looked around. The site ahead of her covered about five acres of cleared land, and in the middle was the remnant of a drilling rig, with the derrick toppled over to the side. Hard to imagine—she shook her head—that this had once been a twenty-five-million-dollar rig.

Huge Caterpillar vehicles dominated the perimeter of the site, and to her right were three trailers. Men stood around in clusters, all wearing brightly colored overalls, hard hats, ear protectors, and safety boots. Capri knew she must stick out like a sore thumb. Yet nobody seemed to have noticed her...

Except for the security guard.

She watched as the burly weatherbeaten man walked purposefully toward her across a sea of mud. He was wearing orange overalls and a white hard hat, with a Blue Spruce Security badge clipped to his breast pocket.

He waited till he was just a couple of feet from Capri before he spoke, but still he had to shout to make himself heard above the din that shook the air around them. "You lookin' for someone, miss?" His pupils expanded as he ran an assessing gaze over the curves revealed by the skintight designer jeans tucked into the top of her leather boots.

Capri nodded, pressing her hands over her ears as she shouted back. "Taggart Smith..."

The man tore his gaze away and glanced briefly at one of the Cats before turning back to Capri. "Lady," he yelled, "Taggart Smith's a mighty busy man right now——"

"I know!" Capri had followed his glance, and, though she could see someone in the cab, she couldn't tell if it was Taggart. "Do you think he'll be much longer?"

The big man bent down, a mocking glint in his eye as he shouted in her ear, "Maybe an hour...maybe two weeks, depending on how long it takes!"

Capri kept her hands pressed against her ears. "I'm going to wait a while," she shouted back. Rummaging in her purse, she extricated the gold case in which she kept her business cards and handed one to the guard. "When you get a chance, will you give him this?"

The guard glanced at the card, and raised his eyebrows as he saw her name and the Jones Oil logo. "You can wait in there." He jerked a thumb toward one of the trailers.

Capri followed him up the steps leading to the trailer, and he pushed the door open and ushered her inside. Several men sat around a table, their attention focused on a chart. The walls were papered with maps, blueprints, and drawings; the windows covered with some kind of insulating material.

One of the men looked round and the guard said, "How about a coffee for the lady, Mac?" He picked up a pair of ear protectors and tossed them to Capri.

"You betcha."

The door slammed shut behind the guard, and the man called Mac poured coffee into a plastic cup.

"That's fine." Capri put on the protectors gratefully as she sat on one of the metal chairs. "I take it black."

He went straight back to the table after handing Capri her drink. She might as well not be there, she realized. She could feel the tension in the trailer, a tension which increased as the men talked among themselves.

"If he can't do it before dark, we should be thinking of setting a second drilling rig. All hell will break loose if the public finds out these poisonous gases are——"

"Yeah."

"If he can't get the blow-out preventer on to the well by...say, six-thirty——"

"That's right. Six-thirty. Or seven. Before it starts getting dark, anyway. We can't do a damn thing after it gets dark. So if he can't, we'll have to——"

"Relight it."

"Yup."

Capri noticed to her amazement that her fingers were steady as she held the coffee mug to her lips. She knew that one breath of concentrated hydrogen sulphide could be lethal, yet somehow she was managing to cope with her worry about Taggart, her terror in case something should happen to him. Would she one day perhaps be able to watch him as he battled to control a raging fire? For the very first time, she believed that yes, one day she might. Oh, not in the near future, but——

Silence.

All at once, the trailer—the whole world!—was filled with silence. A silence that, because of its total unexpectedness, was as shattering, as deafening, as the horrendous noise which had been pounding through the air just a fraction of a second before. But now that noise had stopped.

It took time for human ears to adjust, and during that time, the men at the table froze. Capri did too. She stared unblinkingly at the motionless tableau before her.

And then the tableau dissolved, and it was as if the scene before her was in a movie—one that was being played before her eyes in "fast forward"!

The men spun into action. As one, they ripped off their ear protectors, shoved back their chairs and jumped to their feet. Grabbing up air packs, they made for the door, the floor reverberating under their heavy boots.

As they thundered down the metal steps of the trailer, Capri stared after them, stunned—almost shocked—by the urgency and ruthless efficiency of their movements. In less than five heartbeats, she was alone in the trailer, watching through the open doorway as the men raced to the wellhead to test for minor leaks of the dangerous gas.

She took off her ear protectors, and, propping her elbows on her knees, bent forward and closed her eyes, her brow supported by the heels of her palms. She wasn't sure how long she stayed like that...maybe three or four minutes...while she tried to calm herself. And then she got up, and walked to the door. Leaning against the frame to support her unsteady legs, she searched the site for Taggart. It seemed like an eternity before she spotted him.

But when she did, she felt as if her heart was going to burst.

He was striding—no, *strutting*, like a rooster in a barnyard!—toward one of the other trailers; she had never seen a man walk with such bold self-assurance. Macho, arrogant, godlike—there were no words strong enough to describe him! Despite his crimson overalls and white hard hat, she would have known him anywhere. That confident swagger was unique.

She heard him shout something to the men behind him, heard them laugh. Pride swept through her—it was impossible not to sense the camaraderie that existed between him and the others, a kind of camaraderie which, she sensed, was peculiar to men who worked and risked their lives together.

And as she watched, she saw the security guard approach him, saw something being passed between them...and knew it had to be her business card.

She froze, watching Taggart as he looked at it. Distantly, she heard the breeze rustle through the pine trees behind the trailer, heard the sound of idling engines, felt the edge of the doorframe jut into her shoulder. And then she saw Taggart lift his head sharply, as a wild animal might, who had scented an intruder in his territory...

If only she could see his expression, but her eyes had blurred... What was his reaction going to be? Perhaps he would send a message back by the security guard...perhaps he would tell her he was too busy to talk with her...

And then as she blinked, she saw him detach himself from the others and begin walking toward her.

Not till he was about ten yards from the trailer, his boots squelching noisily in the mud, did she finally manage to move. Her own boots made a tinny, clattering sound on the steps of the trailer as she hurried down them.

His face was caked with mud, and she'd never seen his features so drawn, so utterly exhausted. But his blue eyes, though strained and slightly bloodshot, were still alert. And they gave nothing away.

"Hi." He wiped a tanned hand over his jaw, adding to the grime already there. "You're looking good, Jones."

"You too." And *that*, she thought, had to be the understatement of the year! Tensely, she grasped the strap of her shoulderbag. "You've finished the job?"

"That's right."

"Congratulations."

"Thanks."

"Was this...one of the toughest jobs you've ever handled?"

His shrug was barely noticeable, his blue eyes cool, indifferent. "It was a tough job."

And *that*, she knew, was another understatement! "I'm glad I caught you." Her voice was husky. No games, she told herself; there was no time for games. She was going to put her cards on the table.

"You are?"

She tried to smile, but her lips just wouldn't curve. The moment was too serious, too important. "Remember," she managed, "what you said to me on the island..."

He had never looked so devastatingly male and rugged—nor, she decided apprehensively, had he ever looked quite so hard and unapproachable. "I said quite a few things to you on the island." His voice was low and slightly mocking.

"You said once that the ball was in my court, and the next move was up to me?"

He tilted back his hard hat and Capri noticed that his silky blond hair was now almost black with sweat and dirt. "I thought you made your move," he said evenly, "when you told me you'd hold me forever."

Of course he was right. Capri felt hot shame color her cheeks. She *had* promised him that...but within hours had reneged on her promise. It was quite clear he wasn't going to make things easy. But she could handle that. She had never thought it was going to be easy. "I'd like to make one more move."

She saw his eyebrows rise but he said nothing.

Taking a deep breath, she went on, "I've booked a suite at the Westin Inn..." they were the hardest words she had ever spoken in her life "...and I'll be there tonight."

A muscle twitched in his cheek. "Alone?"

The breeze lifted her jacket, revealing the firm swell of her breasts under her cream sweater. His gaze flickered down, then back to hers. His eyes were darker than they had been a moment before. "I hope not," she said clearly.

He paused for a beat before answering. "And tomorrow?" His expression was guarded. "Will you be alone tomorrow?"

Capri's fingers curled around the strap of her purse. "I hope not." As she looked up at him, she knew that all the love in her heart was shining there for him to see. "I hope I won't be alone tomorrow."

Then drawing on all her courage, she added softly, "I hope I'll never be alone again."

A strange expression flitted over his face—it was so fleeting she wasn't sure how to interpret it but, even as she hesitated, someone hailed him and he glanced over his shoulder. Two men were standing by one of the other trailers, obviously waiting for him. "I'm sorry," he said gently. "I have to go now."

Capri bit her lip. "Taggart...?" The unspoken question trembled in her voice.

"I have a bunch of stuff to do before I'm finished here. Reports to fill in, government officials to see. Then when I get back to town I have an appointment I can't break." The lines fanning from his eyes looked suddenly deeper, his eyes suddenly wearier. "I may not get to my own hotel till late, and by the time I get cleaned up, it——"

"I understand," she interrupted stiffly.

"No, you don't," he said. Unexpectedly, he reached out and brushed the knuckles of his hand over her cheek.

"As I was about to say, by the time I get cleaned up it may be late. Will you wait up for me, Jones? We have to talk."

Talk? Just talk? Capri had shivered at the touch of his knuckle against her heated skin; now she was conscious of a sinking feeling in the pit of her stomach. Was he going to tell her their relationship was over? "Yes," she said as steadily as she could manage. "I'll wait up."

With a quick nod, he turned away, and, without looking back, joined the men waiting for him and disappeared into the other trailer. Capri hesitated for just a moment, and then, forcing her wobbly legs to move, returned to her cab.

As she slid into her seat, she caught a glimpse of her face in the rearview mirror. Her gray-green eyes looked huge, and lost, like the eyes of a waif. And her skin was white as the petals of a snowdrop—the pallor accentuated by the dark smudge of oil which Taggart had left on her cheekbone.

She took a lace-trimmed handkerchief from her bag, bringing a suspicion of Must de Cartier into the stale air of the cab as she did, and wiped the mark away. She looked at the soiled handkerchief for a long moment, then, with an aching heart, she folded it and slid it into the zippered section of her bag.

Depending on what happened tonight, she might keep his handkerchief forever.

For it might be her only tangible reminder of Taggart Smith.

CHAPTER TWELVE

"MISS JONES," the hotel clerk's voice on the telephone was discreet, "I have a Mr. Smith for you in the front lobby."

"Thank you. Send him up, please."

Capri glanced at her watch as she shakily replaced the receiver. Ten to eleven. Had Taggart expected he would be this late? She hadn't. She had almost given up hope that he was coming—had almost decided he had changed his mind.

Feeling her heart thumping against her ribs, she got up off the edge of the bed, and, slipping on her black high-heeled shoes, made her way through to the reception room.

The faint fragrance of Must de Cartier drifted to her nostrils as she ran trembling hands through her tumbled hair. She had showered on her return to the hotel, and had chosen to wear a black cashmere dress which clung sensually to every feminine curve.

When she heard the firm knock on the door, she felt a jolt of apprehension that almost knocked her knees from under her. Playing nervously with her watch, she walked across the foyer.

Her stomach muscles clenched. Relax, she ordered herself, as she pulled back the chain and opened the door.

"Good evening, Capri."

He was dressed the way he had been on that last afternoon on the island, when he'd left on the chopper. His masculinity dazzled her, making her blink the way she did when sunlight danced in her eyes. Awkwardly, she stepped back. "Come in."

As she hung his jacket in the cupboard, she smelled he male scent of him lingering on the soft leather, and he unexpectedness of it threw her off balance. She stood or a long moment, steadying herself, barely aware that Taggart had moved through to the reception area and across to the bar. The only sound in the hushed silence vas the splash of liquid as he poured drinks.

Was his to be "one for the road"?

Her gaze became blurred, and, after she brushed away he threatening tears with the back of one hand, she noticed that Taggart had slid back the door to the balcony, and had gone to stand outside in the dark. As he moved to join him, she felt her nerves tighten to napping point.

The night air smelled of the city—but, looking up at his man she loved, at his tousled blond hair and rugged features, Capri could almost smell again the fragrance of the ocean, and the wildflowers of Blueberry Island. The bittersweet memories were almost too painful to bear.

"Quite a view, isn't it?" he murmured. He held out her drink, and as she took it their fingers brushed together. Her eyelids flickered as electricity jumped between them.

"Yes, it is. Quite a view." The mass of twinkling lights seemed to stretch for ever. "I'm glad you were able to make it."

He looked down at her and his eyes glinted in the dark. "You took me by surprise this afternoon."

The cool breeze lifted her hair and blew a few strands over her face. Abstractedly, she anchored them behind her ear. "I'm sorry... perhaps I should have tried to contact you via your office, rather than go out to the site..."

"If you had, you might have missed me. I had already tentatively booked a seat on the midnight flight out of own."

Capri felt her heart tremble. Was he still planning t
leave on that flight? Had he come to say goodbye? Ha
their interlude on Blueberry been, for him, just a summe
affair after all? Her throat tightened so she could hardl
swallow.

"It was good of you to come by, then," she someho
managed, "but I won't keep you——"

"I was hoping you would."

"Would...what?"

"Keep me." Without taking his eyes from her, h
placed his drink on the balcony railing. "I was hop
ing——" his voice had become low and husky "—tha
you would keep me forever."

Disbelief swept through Capri. Had he really said wha
she thought he had said? "But your midnight flight...
She bit her lip as he took her glass and placed it alongsid
his own. "Aren't you going away?"

"Come here." Taggart held out his arms and Cap
walked into them, feeling as if she was in a dream. B
as Taggart's embrace enfolded her she realized it was n
dream. The steel-hard strength of his muscles was fa
too real...far too familiar...to be part of any dream

"Away?" he said. "No, I'm not going away." He hel
her a little from him, and the intensity of his emotio
made his eyes as dark as the sky above. "That's wha
you want, isn't it—that we'll be together for always?"

Capri felt her heart soar, felt as if she was floatin
heavenward as joy exploded inside her. "Oh, ye
Taggart, that's what I want!"

The smile he bestowed on her was like no other smi
she had ever seen. It was as tender, and as imbued wit
promise, as the first day of spring. "Then that, m
darling Jones, is what you shall have." Tangling on
hand in her hair, he cupped her head with the other, an
tilted her face up to his.

The tiny moan that sprang to life in Capri's thro
was smothered as his lips captured her own in a kiss th

ent shivers sizzling right to the tips of her pink-frosted
oenails. She slid her arms around his neck and laced
ter fingers together, delighting in the silky texture of his
olond hair. Then, with a sigh of surrender, she gave
aerself up completely to the exquisite pleasure surging
o powerfully through her...

A long time later, Taggart murmured, "I want babies,
Capri." His voice was husky with yearning.

Capri clung to him weakly. "I know, my darling...and
o do I. Lots of them..."

His hands moved to her back, where they caressed her
possessively, lingering over the seductive softness of the
olack cashmere. "I know your career is important to
ou. I want you to have that too. I want you to have
everything, my love, everything that it's in my power to
give you."

With a bemused smile, Capri recalled the picture she'd
once visualized of herself running up the steps of Jones
Oil with a blue-eyed blond baby in her arms. Now she
aw another picture—oh, she still had a baby in her arms,
but there was a toddler hopping up the steps beside her
nd also a——

The day care report! She had forgotten all about it!
She would have to present it at the October board
meeting instead...

"I'll start my own company—based in Houston,"
Taggart murmured. "And I'll build you the house of
our dreams—with a nursery and lots of bedrooms. We'll
spend our holidays on Blueberry, and our children will
olay there on the beach. But sometimes we'll let the
randparents look after them, and we'll go to our cabin
alone..."

"It's going to take some time to fill all those bed-
ooms." Capri looked up at him mischievously from be-
eath her long lashes. "Do you have any suggestions as
o when we should get started?"

A teasing spark shimmered in his desire-dark eye "Just can't wait, can you, Jones? I've spent the past tw weeks coping with one raging fire ... and now you wa me to walk right into another one! Oh, well, never l it be said that I don't know how to treat a lady!"

Capri uttered a blissful sigh as, with an ominou chuckle, he swept her up in his arms and strode towar the bedroom. Oh, Taggart Smith knew *exactly* how 1 treat a lady!

And she knew beyond the shadow of a doubt tha no matter what the future might bring, she would neve once regret the risk she had taken.

Her risk of the heart.

WELCOME TO

The quintessential small town where everyone knows everybody else!

Finally, books that capture the pleasure of tuning in to your favorite TV show!

GREAT READING...GREAT SAVINGS...AND A FABULOUS FREE GIFT!

Each book set in Tyler is a self-contained love story; together, the twelve novels stitch the fabric of the community. The covers honor the old American tradition of quilting; each cover depicts a patch of the large Tyler quilt.

With Tyler you can receive a fabulous gift ABSOLUTELY FREE by collecting proofs-of-purchase found in each Tyler book. And use our special Tyler coupons to save on your next TYLER book purchase.

Join your friends at Tyler for the sixth book, SUNSHINE by Pat Warren, available in August.

When Janice Eber becomes a widow, does her husband's friend David provide more than just friendship?

Back by Popular Demand

Janet Dailey
Americana

Janet Dailey takes you on a romantic tour of
America through fifty favorite Harlequin
Presents novels, each one set in a different
state, and researched by Janet and her husband,
Bill.

A journey of a lifetime. The perfect collectable
series!

August titles **#37 OREGON**
To Tell the Truth

#38 PENNSYLVANIA
The Thawing of Mara

If you missed your state or would like to order any other states that
have already been published, send your name, address, zip or postal
code, along with a check or money order for $3.99 (please do not send
cash), plus 75¢ postage and handling ($1.00 in Canada) for each book
ordered, payable to Harlequin Reader Service to:

In the U.S.	In Canada
3010 Walden Avenue	P.O. Box 609
P.O. Box 1325	Fort Erie, Ontario
Buffalo, NY 14269-1325	L2A 5X3

Available at retail outlets in the U.S. only.
Please specify book title(s) with your order.
Canadian residents add applicable federal and provincial taxes. JD-AUG

JAYNE ANN KRENTZ

A two-part epic tale from one of today's most popular romance novelists!

Dreams
Parts One & Two

The warrior died at her feet, his blood running out of the cave entrance and mingling with the waterfall. With his last breath he cursed the woman— told her that her spirit would remain chained in the cave forever until a child was created and born there....

So goes the ancient legend of the Chained Lady and the curse that bound her throughout the ages—until destiny brought Diana Prentice and Colby Savager together under the influence of forces beyond their understanding. Suddenly they were both haunted by dreams that linked past and present, while their waking hours were filled with danger. Only when Colby, Diana's modern-day warrior, learned to love, could those dark forces be vanquished. Only then could Diana set the Chained Lady free....

Harlequin Intrigue ®

43 Light St.

It looks like a charming old building near the Baltimore waterfront, but inside 43 Light Street lurks danger ... and romance.

Labeled a "true master of intrigue" by *Rave Reviews*, bestselling author Rebecca York continues her exciting series with TRIAL BY FIRE, coming to you next month.

Sabrina Barkley, owner of an herbal shop at 43 Light Street, finds that the past has a bizarre way of affecting the present when she's called in by ADA Dan Cassidy to consult on a murder case—only to be herself accused of murder *and* witchcraft. Sabrina's only defense is four hundred years old and an ocean away....

Watch for TRIAL BY FIRE in August, and all the upcoming 43 Light Street titles for top-notch suspense and romance.

LS92-1

OFFICIAL RULES • MILLION DOLLAR MATCH 3 SWEEPSTAKES
NO PURCHASE OR OBLIGATION NECESSARY TO ENTER

To enter, follow the directions published. If the "Match 3" Game Card is missing, hand print your name and address on a 3″×5″ card and mail to either: Harlequin "Match 3," 3010 Walden Ave., P.O. Box 1867, Buffalo, NY 14269-1867 or Harlequin "Match 3," P.O. Box 609, Fort Erie, Ontario L2A 5X3, and we will assign your Sweepstakes numbers. (Limit: one entry per envelope.) For eligibility, entries must be received no later than March 31, 1994 and be sent via first-class mail. No liability is assumed for printing errors, lost, late or misdirected entries.

Upon receipt of entry, Sweepstakes numbers will be assigned. To determine winners, Sweepstakes numbers will be compared against a list of randomly preselected prizewinning numbers. In the event all prizes are not claimed via the return of prizewinning numbers, random drawings will be held from among all other entries received to award unclaimed prizes.

Prizewinners will be determined no later than May 30, 1994. Selection of winning numbers and random drawings are under the supervision of D.L. Blair, Inc., an independent judging organization, whose decisions are final. One prize to a family or organization. No substitution will be made for any prize, except as offered. Taxes and duties on all prizes are the sole responsibility of winners. Winners will be notified by mail. Chances of winning are determined by the number of entries distributed and received.

Sweepstakes open to persons 18 years of age or older, except employees and immediate family members of Torstar Corporation, D.L. Blair, Inc., their affiliates, subsidiaries and all other agencies, entities and persons connected with the use, marketing or conduct of this Sweepstakes. All applicable laws and regulations apply. Sweepstakes offer void wherever prohibited by law. Any litigation within the province of Quebec respecting the conduct and awarding of a prize in this Sweepstakes must be submitted to the Régies des Loteries et Courses du Quebec. In order to win a prize, residents of Canada will be required to correctly answer a time-limited arithmetical skill-testing question. Values of all prizes are in U.S. currency.

Winners of major prizes will be obligated to sign and return an affidavit of eligibility and release of liability within 30 days of notification. In the event of non-compliance within this time period, prize may be awarded to an alternate winner. Any prize or prize notification returned as undeliverable will result in the awarding of that prize to an alternate winner. By acceptance of their prize, winners consent to use of their names, photographs or other likenesses for purposes of advertising, trade and promotion on behalf of Torstar Corporation without further compensation, unless prohibited by law.

This Sweepstakes is presented by Torstar Corporation, its subsidiaries and affiliates in conjunction with book, merchandise and/or product offerings. Prizes are as follows: Grand Prize—$1,000,000 (payable at $33,333.33 a year for 30 years). First through Sixth Prizes may be presented in different creative executions, each with the following appproximate values: First Prize—$35,000; Second Prize—$10,000; 2 Third Prizes—$5,000 each; 5 Fourth Prizes—$1,000 each; 10 Fifth Prizes—$250 each; 1,000 Sixth Prizes—$100 each. Prizewinners will have the opportunity of selecting any prize offered for that level. A travel-prize option, if offered and selected by winner, must be completed within 12 months of selection and is subject to hotel and flight accommodations availability. Torstar Corporation may present this Sweepstakes utilizing names other than Million Dollar Sweepstakes. For a current list of all prize options offered within prize levels and all names the Sweepstakes may utilize, send a self-addressed, stamped envelope (WA residents need not affix return postage) to: Million Dollar Sweepstakes Prize Options/Names, P.O. Box 4710, Blair, NE 68009.

For a list of prizewinners (available after July 31, 1994) send a separate, stamped, self-addressed envelope to: Million Dollar Sweepstakes Winners, P.O. Box 4728, Blair, NE 68009.   MSW7-92